FINDING JADE

FINDING JADE

MARY JENNIFER PAYNE

Daughters of Light

DUNDURN
TORONTO

Cover image: © Armin Staudt/ istockphoto.com
Printer: Webcom

Library and Archives Canada Cataloguing in Publication

Payne, Mary Jennifer, author
        Finding Jade / Mary Jennifer Payne.

Issued in print and electronic formats.

ISBN 978-1-4597-3500-2 (paperback).--ISBN 978-1-4597-3501-9 (pdf).--
ISBN 978-1-4597-3502-6 (epub)

        I. Title.

PS8631.A9543F55 2016   C813'.6   C2016-900230-6
                                               C2016-900231-4

1   2   3   4   5   20   19   18   17   16

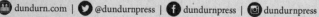
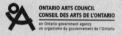

Conseil des Arts   Canada Council
du Canada   for the Arts

ONTARIO ARTS COUNCIL
CONSEIL DES ARTS DE L'ONTARIO
an Ontario government agency
un organisme du gouvernement de l'Ontario

We acknowledge the support of the **Canada Council for the Arts** and the **Ontario Arts Council** for our publishing program. We also acknowledge the financial support of the **Government of Ontario**, through the **Ontario Book Publishing Tax Credit** and the **Ontario Media Development Corporation**, and the **Government of Canada**.

VISIT US AT

 dundurn.com | 🐦 @dundurnpress | f dundurnpress | 📷 dundurnpress

Dundurn
3 Church Street, Suite 500
Toronto, Ontario, Canada
M5E 1M2

To Robert — for making every moment brighter

CHAPTER 1

It's my first day of grade nine. I'm standing at the front desk in the office at Riverdale, my new high school.

And I think I'm losing my mind again.

"But this is where I'm supposed to go," I say. I pull out my acceptance letter, hand it to the secretary, and plaster a smile across my face. As Mom always says, "You can catch more flies with honey than with vinegar."

"Sorry, Jasmine," the secretary begins, sliding the letter back across the desk at me. There's this massive silver ring with a weird, blue-sky coloured stone on her right index finger. I can't help staring at it. "You need to attend Beaconsfield. They're expecting you."

I can't believe it. My acceptance letter is sitting there on the desk, complete with a cheesy welcome message from the principal. It's pretty obvious I've been accepted to this school, but she's refusing to even look at the letter.

"But I'm supposed to go here." I point at the acceptance box, which is clearly ticked with a black check mark. Every last atom in my body is shrieking with rage. I want to shout at this woman, but know doing that will only make things worse — if they can get any worse.

I slide the letter toward her again. My hands are shaking. I feel like a volcano that's ready to blow. The morning bell rings.

"Beaconsfield is that new school, right?" I ask through gritted teeth. "It's at least a twenty-minute bus ride from here. There's no way I'm supposed to go there."

"You'll attend Beaconsfield," she says flatly, running her well-manicured fingers through her bleached hair.

"Can I speak to someone else about this, then?" I ask, digging my nails into the fleshy part of my palm to keep from screaming. I look down. Tiny crescent-shaped nail marks dent my skin.

"Sorry. Everyone else is busy."

That's when I notice that the office is nearly empty. Other than this weirdo secretary, there's just an elderly caretaker dumping out wastepaper baskets into a large garbage bag. And he doesn't even seem to notice us.

I open the office door and check the hallway to see if my friends Desiree and Aisha are waiting for me. Maybe they'll have better luck convincing this insane woman to let me into class. But they've already gone to their home-room classes, likely thinking I'd be right behind them.

I go back in and glare at the secretary. This is so stupid. I practically live around the corner. There's no way I can be out of district or anything like that.

"Okay," I say, "I'll call my mom. Believe me, she's going to come down here and lose it if you tell her everyone's too busy to see her." I fold my arms across my chest and wait for her reaction.

The secretary gives me this little knowing smile, like we're sharing a secret, like she somehow knows that Mom is in the hospital getting treatment right now and can't be reached.

Then she takes off her black-framed glasses, rests her forearms on the desk, and leans toward me as if she's about to share her deepest, darkest secrets.

"Jasmine, you have no choice in this matter. You must go to Beaconsfield," she says, her tone serious. I want to ask who died and made her God, but I don't think that would go over very well.

"Come on," I say. "You know not letting me in is crazy. I live, like, two minutes away. Kids from my junior high always go here."

"We're done having this discussion." Her calm attitude makes the situation even more infuriating.

I pick up the letter and rattle it in her face. "Can't you read?" I shout.

The woman shakes her head. "Go to Beaconsfield, Jasmine," she says, before getting up and walking across the room to the photocopier.

Dumbfounded, I snatch my knapsack off the floor, open the zipper, and stuff my acceptance letter inside. I'm so angry I want to kick things. Instead, I fling open the office door so that it hits the brick wall behind it with a satisfying bang and storm out.

Then I reluctantly make my way to Beaconsfield Collegiate.

It's only as I'm climbing the stone steps to enter Beaconsfield that I realize something. The secretary hadn't even looked at my acceptance letter. So how did she know my name?

CHAPTER 2

One thing you need to know about me is that I detest speaking in class. When I have to, even if it is just to give a quick answer, it's like my voice freezes up and my brain stops working. Sometimes I even stutter. These days I only seem to be able to find my voice when I'm angry. Thing is, I wasn't always this awkward. It's something that started after my twin sister, Jade, disappeared.

That's why I hate the first day of school. Every single teacher alive seems to think making students introduce themselves is a great idea. Like we care. We'll figure out the names of the people we actually want to talk to soon enough.

I was hoping, considering it was practically mid-morning before I got to Beaconsfield, that all of this first day, ice-breaker garbage would be done and over with by the time I entered a classroom. No such luck.

As my turn gets closer, any hint of moisture in my mouth immediately leaves and travels to my palms. I wipe my hands on my jeans and practise what I'm going to say in my head.

Hi. My name is Jasmine Guzman. My mother is dying a slow, painful death, and my sister, Jade, was abducted when we were ten years old. Soon I will be an orphan. P.S.: My sister's body was never found.

Yeah, I know. But I'd love to say that and just watch the look on the teacher's face. You asked us to tell you something important about ourselves, right? Well, here it is. Still think your little introduction game is great?

This teacher, Mr. Khan, looks pretty young. It's probably his first year teaching and some old fart likely gave him this idea about the stupid-ass introductions. One way you can tell that a teacher is just starting out in their career and wants to make a good impression is by the way they dress. Khan wears a sharply pressed blue-striped dress shirt and a tie that looks brand new. I'll admit I like his hair. It's so black it's almost blue, and he has it kind of spiked. He isn't bad looking either, just way too eager. Teachers that have been kicking around for a long time never dress like Mr. Khan. Those dinosaurs usually wear something that looks like it was picked out of a laundry hamper in 2004 and never washed again. Sometimes they even have chicory stains on their shirts or enough cat hair on their clothing to kill a kid with allergies. Gross.

Eventually my turn comes around, and, as usual, I can barely choke out my name.

"Hi." My face is as hot as a chicken on a rotisserie spit. "I'm …" My vocal cords have constricted, turning my voice into a frog-like croak. Now I'm getting pained looks of sympathy from some of my classmates and Mr. Khan. "Jasmine … Guzman."

A loud snicker comes from the girl with the long, mahogany-coloured hair sitting directly behind me. Great.

"Would you like to tell us anything else about yourself, Jasmine?" Mr. Khan interjects. Clearly, he's trying to save me from further embarrassment.

I shake my head, not trusting my voice.

"Well, welcome," he says, shooting me one of those overly enthusiastic smiles that teachers who really enjoy their jobs seem to always have in reserve.

"Yeah, welcome, midget," the girl behind me says quietly.

"Did you have something you wanted to share with the class, Mina?" Mr. Khan asks. He leans his slender frame against his desk and casually tosses a tablet stylus up and down in the palm of his right hand.

"Well, actually …" the girl begins. Her voice oozes confidence. I'm not about to turn around, but can visualize in my head the smug smile she's wearing. "Most of you know me, of course. Mina James for those of you who might not. Something important? I was in a music video this summer. Nothing big. You might have seen it on Music Online. Just a little something with me dancing for Drizzy Junior."

She's getting looks of admiration mingled with a bit of awe and fear. Okay, not only am I the shortest person in this homeroom, but it seems like I might be the target of bullying by the popular and pretty girl who just happens to dance in videos for the hottest rapper ever in her spare time.

As the next person introduces himself to the class, Mina leans in close to me. I don't turn around; I'm not going to give her that satisfaction.

"Just stay out of my way, midget," she hisses. "I don't want you around me in case your ugliness is contagious."

I don't say anything. As far as I'm concerned, me even being at this school is a massive mistake — one that Mom will hopefully sort out tomorrow. I wonder how Desiree and Aisha are doing. They're probably freaking out, wondering what happened to me.

As the introductions continue, I notice something strange. There are five sets of identical twins in our class. Okay, I know all about fertility treatments and the spike in twins because of them, but this is too weird. And what's even weirder is the fact that all of the twins are girls. What kind of a freak-show school is this?

When the day ends, I immediately contact Desiree. It's hard to hear her over the passing cars and city trams, but I can't wait until I get home to talk to her. I need to let her know the hell I've been through.

"Where have you been?" she asks as soon as she picks up. "Check your video messages much?"

"That crazy secretary wouldn't let me in," I explain, holding my video watch to one ear while cupping my free hand over my other ear to hear better. "She said I was enrolled at Beaconsfield, and she sent me here."

"That's insane. There's no way you're supposed to go there," Desiree says. "You're not even in district. And why am I suddenly staring inside your ear?"

I stop to sit on a bench outside a shabby chicory shop. There's a group of cab drivers chatting nearby, and they turn to gaze expectantly at me. I shake my head to let them know I'm not going to be their next fare.

"I know that and you know that," I say, moving my watch back to show my face. "But someone needs to tell the crazy, bleach-blond secretary that. She wouldn't even look at my acceptance letter. What a bitch."

There's a pause from Desiree. "Jazz, the secretary at our school has long, brown hair," she finally says. "And she's the one who registered both me and Aisha. No one else was at the desk."

My stomach drops like an out-of-control elevator while my mind races back to this morning. Okay, Desiree and Aisha were in line ahead of me. Then they each talked to the secretary, but I couldn't really see what she looked like because they were standing in front of me, kind of blocking my view. They registered with no problem and were given their timetables. I told them I'd see them in a minute, and then, when I turned around, the crazy secretary was standing at the desk. I remember she'd had this weird look of anticipation on her face before I even said anything.

And she knew my name.

How is any of this possible?

My hand drops from my face.

"Jasmine?" Desiree says, waving at me from the video screen. "Hello?"

"Yeah," I reply. My voice sounds tiny and far away. "I'll get hold of you later, okay? I need to get some things for Mom before going home."

I end the call and stand up. My palms are sweaty with fear. After talking to Desiree, I'm sure I'm going insane again.

CHAPTER 3

I don't know about you, but I'm never certain what I'm going to find when I get home at the end of a school day. There must be other kids that feel the same way I do: ones whose parents have drinking or drug problems or live with domestic abuse. They probably hate the thought of coming home and finding a parent strung out and lying on the couch, or nursing a black eye. I don't worry about anything like that.

My mom has a disease called lupus. She's had it for a while now, and it's awful. Basically, Mom's body is attacking the healthy parts of itself, and it's killing her. At first she was just really tired, and still had some really good days. Then the disease attacked her joints, causing her hip to hurt so much that she needs a cane to walk now. But the worst thing of all is that the disease is causing her kidneys to fail. She has to go to the hospital for dialysis a few times a week just to stay alive. We're waiting for a kidney donor, and I really hope that we find one soon. Otherwise, I'm going to lose my mom, and she's the only family I have left.

So, because of the lupus, I never know when I walk into our apartment if Mom is going to be feeling really awful or not. Sometimes I worry she might be dead.

By the time I reach the landing outside our apartment, beads of sweat cover my forehead. We live on the tenth floor, and the elevator is out again. To top it off, despite the fact that we're already a week into September, the sun is still scorching hot, and temperatures continue to hover in the mid-forties. I'm in good shape because I like to run, but today I'm carrying bags of carrots, potatoes, and onions, so the stairs nearly kill me. Dealing with the heavy cloud of smog outside hasn't helped, either.

Not that the air inside is much better. People let their dogs piss in the stairwells rather than taking them outside, and, occasionally, drunks decide to use the stairs as their personal toilets as well.

I put the groceries down on the worn tile outside our door and rub my hands together, trying to get rid of the white indentations criss-crossing my fingers and palms where the handles of the bags dug into my skin. Then I take a deep breath, unlock the door, and go inside.

"Is that you, Jasmine?" Mom calls. The apartment is dark except for a faint light from the living room. Mom's probably been on the couch since getting home from her treatment. I hate that I can't be home sooner to help her when she's like this.

"Yeah," I say, nudging the hall light on with my elbow and kicking off my silver ballet flats. "Was Lola here?"

Mom's friend Mopelola, or Lola for short, is the only other person who comes to our apartment anymore.

"She dropped me off a few hours ago," Mom replies. "But she has to work tonight and couldn't stay. She told me to tell you she owes you a hug."

I smile to myself. Lola is nearly six feet tall and always wrapping me in these massive octopus-like hugs whenever she sees me. I tell her I hate it, but secretly, I love those hugs and she knows it.

I drop the bags off in the kitchen on my way to the living room. Mom is lying on the couch with a thin, blue fleece blanket pulled over her and a pillow from her bed behind her head. The curtains are closed. A small table lamp beside her casts a gentle light over her face. She looks small lying there, so small and fragile it makes me want to cry.

"Stupid elevator is out of service again," I say, sitting down on the blood-red velvet armchair opposite the couch. Despite its polka-dotted pattern of moth holes, the chair is still my favourite piece of furniture. Instead of turning on more lights, I let my eyes adjust to the shadowiness of the room. Bright light can give Mom headaches when she's feeling particularly tired.

Mom smiles as she pulls herself up onto her elbows. "Someone's cranky. Bad day?"

Before I can answer, my lungs spasm, and my body is thrown into a fit of coughing.

"You didn't wear your mask, did you?" she asks, her gaze darkening with concern.

I shake my head, unable to answer. Between coughs, I'm trying to gulp down mouthfuls of air like a dying goldfish. A few years ago, the government began giving out masks to help people breathe when pollution levels get über-high, like today. Of course, they only did so after young children and the elderly began dropping like flies. At that point it was pretty much impossible for our leaders to continue denying the existence of climate change.

Holding up a finger to signal that I'll be right back, I go to the kitchen to pour myself a glass of water. After a few gulps, my coughing subsides. I go back and sit beside Mom on the sofa.

I explain to her what happened with the secretary and about being sent to Beaconsfield. Though I hate giving her anything extra to worry about, I really need her to talk to someone at the school and sort things out.

She frowns. "That doesn't seem right at all. I'll call first thing tomorrow. And if they don't resolve the situation, Lola and I will drive over to Riverdale, and I'll personally speak to them. Especially that secretary."

I get up and give her a gentle hug. "Thanks, Mom. You're the best."

"I know," she says with a smile. "Now, what feast are you preparing for our dinner?"

"How about some veggie empanadas?"

"*Deliciosa*," Mom replies as she lies back down on the pillow. There are dark, bruise-like circles under her eyes, and her cheeks are red and rashy. I feel terrible for telling her about the mix-up at school. It's clear she's having one of her bad days.

Back in the kitchen, I take out eggs and flour for the empanada dough and put the carrots and potatoes in a bowl to be washed and peeled. Dinner is going to take some prep time, but I needed something that was pretty cheap to make with ingredients we could keep using until Mom's disability cheque arrives at the end of the week.

I walk over to get the chopping board at the other end of the counter and twist my ankle as I step on something hard.

"Damn!" I cry out, my arms pinwheeling in an attempt to keep my balance.

A little wooden statue skitters out from under my foot and across the floor. Its features are oversized: big eyes, huge head, prominent lips and nose. The only other details are some type of headdress and what may be a beaded necklace around the doll's thick neck. It looks a lot like the African art and carvings I've seen in Lola's apartment.

I squat down and pick it up.

A cracking thunderclap fills my ears. My heart nearly stops as a surge of energy flashes into my hand, up my arm, and back down my spine. It feels like white lightning. Nausea rolls over me. My body shakes uncontrollably as a series of images flood my mind like a tsunami; it's as if a movie is being downloaded into my brain. I drop the statue and fall backward, smashing my back against the kitchen cupboards as I land.

I stare wide-eyed at the statue, which is now lying on the chipped linoleum just to my right. My body is still shaking, so I take a few deep breaths to try and calm myself.

"Jasmine?" Mom is standing in the doorway, leaning heavily on her cane. "Are you okay?"

"I tripped over that," I say, pointing at the statue. "But, yeah, I'm okay."

Mom slowly makes her way over to me. "Are you sure you're all right? That sounded like a hard fall. The way you screamed nearly gave me a heart attack."

I screamed? My mind is a blank.

Mom walks to the statue. It's clear the effort of moving just a few metres fatigues her.

"Oh, that's Lola's," she says. "She must've dropped it when she was here today." She stoops to pick it up.

"Don't!" I say, reaching out for her arm.

Mom wraps her hand around the wooden doll's enormous head, slowly straightens, and looks at me, her brows drawing together in a frown.

"Sure you're okay?" she asks as she places the statue on the counter.

I get up and self-consciously brush my hands along the front of my jeans. "I just didn't want you to pick it up, that's all. You should be resting." It's true. I feel badly that Mom has exerted all this energy because I'm dumb enough to scream over a piece of wood. It probably just gave me a static electric shock or something. Usually, I'd never let her pick something up off the floor, let alone be up and walking around after a treatment.

Admittedly, I am happy I didn't have to touch that thing again.

After dinner I finish the dishes and then slip away to my room. As I'm lying on the bed, reading from my tablet, I suddenly remember what I saw during the seconds I had touched Lola's doll.

There's no way it was anything but a hallucination of some sort, yet it was so vivid, so real....

I get up, cross the room, open the closet door, and rummage around until my fingers hit the treasure box. It might sound stupid to have a treasure box at my age, but it was something that Jade and I started the year before she disappeared. We created it just after Mom told us how our dad died and about their life together in Chile.

The box initially started as a little dedication to him. Eventually, it turned into a place for us to store all our shared treasures: favourite shells collected at the beach, First Communion necklaces, dried flowers we picked from neighbourhood gardens when no one was looking, and a photo of our parents taken in Valparaíso when they were just teenagers. Then, after Jade disappeared, I began to add things to it that reminded me of her. In the deepest place of my heart, I hoped one day she'd come back, so I could share the box with her.

Jade was the only other person who knew about the box. In the last year or so I finally accepted that she was gone, and I've kept it hidden at the back of my closet ever since, buried under piles of old clothes I grew out of long ago.

Hands shaking, I pull it out. It's just an old shoebox covered with silver and pink glitter-glue flowers and pictures of cats and dogs that Jade and I cut out from magazines. We always wanted a pet of our own, but Mom's allergic.

I lift the lid. Nothing's been touched in so long. I pull out a photo of Jade smiling widely at the camera, singing into a banana she was using as a substitute microphone at school. It was taken just a few months before her disappearance. She loved singing and dancing, and was always talking about how one day she'd star in musicals in the biggest theatres from here to New York and London. It used to drive me nuts, but now I'd do anything to hear her sing again. Underneath that photo is the cloth napkin we stole from a dinner at a fancy restaurant when our *abuela* came to visit from Chile. The edges of the fabric are yellowing slightly. Picking up the photo of Jade again, I think about the vision I had when I touched Lola's wooden doll.

Included in the jumble of horrific images that I saw when I touched the doll was one vision that struck me to the core. For a few fleeting seconds, I saw Jade. She was running and seemed terrified. Not only that, she was no longer ten years old, but looked a lot like I do now at fourteen.

I stare at my sister's huge smile a few moments longer, put the photo back at the very bottom of the box, and lean back against the door frame of my closet.

What's happening to me?

And, though I don't want to go near the doll again, something tells me not to leave it unguarded.

I wait until Mom is asleep before heading back to the kitchen. Using a pair of tongs, I carefully pick up Lola's doll from the counter, walk back to my room and place it in the box.

CHAPTER 4

Mom wouldn't let me stay home from school today, which means I'm back at Beaconsfield until she can sort out this whole stupid mess.

"Jasmine, can you please read to the class the first paragraph of your persuasive letter to the editor?" Mr. Khan asks. We're nearly through second period. I look up at him, wishing his handsome head would spontaneously combust.

"No, thanks," I say, keeping my voice low.

The only response I get is a snicker from Mina, who's sitting directly across from me — even though Mr. Khan posted a seating plan this morning that had her sitting nowhere near me. Why doesn't he ask her to move to her assigned seat? Is he afraid of her as well?

"Jasmine? Please begin to read," he says. "You did such an excellent job in your writing yesterday addressing both sides of the debate as to whether or not the execution of climate change terrorists from Los Angeles should be live-streamed."

I shake my head. "I don't want to."

A tiny muscle in Mr. Khan's jaw begins to twitch. Clearly, my reluctance to read is beginning to irritate him.

"Hurry up and read, Ugly," Mina hisses. "You're wasting our time."

I can feel her eyes on me, but I'm not going to even look over because I know that's what she wants. I won't give her the satisfaction of a reaction, even though what I really want to do is put my fist through her face.

"Mina, please," Mr. Khan says, his voice calm. "Go ahead, Jasmine."

He's not going to give up. I glare at him and turn my tablet on.

"Dear Editor: I'm writing you to express my dismay at the decision of the majority of the world's governments, including Canada's, to …"

A loud, dramatic sneeze interrupts my reading. A few people burst out laughing. I want to die.

"Sorry," Mina says coyly. "I must be allergic to something in the room."

"If you're so smart, why don't *you* read *your* work to the class, Mina?"

Shocked, I look up at Mr. Khan. His lips aren't moving. So who's daring to stand up to Mina?

"Could you even understand the topic? Or did you get your friends to explain it to you?"

Like something straight out of an old-fashioned Bollywood movie, every head — including Mina's — turns in unison to look at the source of the voice. It's a boy at the back of the class.

"You're dead," Mina says to him, her eyes narrowing.

"That's enough, you two," Mr. Khan warns.

"I'm *dead*?" the boy chuckles, linking his hands behind his head and leaning back in his seat. A confident smirk plays across his face. I can't take my eyes off him, and I don't know if it's because he's so incredibly ballsy or so stunningly gorgeous. Either way, I'm loving every minute of this showdown.

"You're funny, Mina. A natural comedienne."

"I said that's enough, Raphael," Mr. Khan says. "Everyone in our class has their unique strengths and needs. You know that." He picks up the remote off his desk. "We're almost out of time, so I'll conclude with another news podcast for you to respond to tonight for homework." There's a collective groan as he projects the link onto one of the classroom's monitors.

It turns out Raphael is in my next class, too. Instead of paying attention (which I should since it's math and I'm crap at it), I can't help stealing furtive glances at him. He's got thick, black hair, skin the colour of milky coffee, and eyes that seem to change from the most vivid green to deep brown, depending on how the light from the window is hitting his face.

What I can't understand is why no one else seems to think it's strange that he was suddenly sitting back there during Mr. Khan's lesson last period. We all came into class together, and I was one of the first to sit down. Believe me, there's no way a guy this beautiful could have walked by without me noticing.

Yet no one, including Mr. Khan, appeared to be surprised by his presence. And the freakiest thing is, despite not being in class yesterday, Raphael knows everything we're doing. Either he's a genius or this is yet another crazy thing I can't explain — like this school's creepy identical-twin situation. Today I counted four more pairs of twins during transitions between classes. All girls.

To tell the truth, all this weirdness is beginning to scare me. I wonder if I'm having seizures or something. Could I be blanking out for a few minutes and not realizing it? That might explain me missing things like Raphael entering the classroom. Except that wouldn't explain what happened with Lola's doll.

I decide not to think about it, and try to force my mind to focus on algebraic equations instead. But soon I'm doodling on my page, and my gaze is drifting back to Raphael.

Toward the end of class, he looks up and catches me practically staring at him. My face burns. Before I can look away, he smiles knowingly, like we're sharing some kind of secret. For the second time today, I nearly die of embarrassment.

The rest of my day is pretty good, though, and Mina leaves me alone. I wonder if Raphael calling her out will be enough to stop her from bullying me. Not that it really matters; after today I won't have to worry about seeing any of them again. Although a part of me wishes I could take Raphael to Riverdale with me. I hope there are some hot guys over there. I'll have to ask Desiree.

I clear out my locker at the end of the day and put my lock into my knapsack. *Good riddance,* I think as I slam the door shut. My heart jumps. Mr. Khan is standing on the other side.

"I hear you're hoping to leave us, Jasmine," he says. His voice is full of disappointment.

"Well, yeah. I'm not really supposed to be here," I say, throwing my knapsack over my shoulder and onto my back. "Big mistake over at Riverdale. My mom went to sort it out today. She's asking them to start me on Monday."

"What makes you think this isn't the place you're meant to be?" Mr. Khan leans his shoulder against the locker, as if he's getting ready to have a long conversation.

Newsflash, I think. *I'm outta here.*

"I was accepted at Riverdale," I say with a shrug. "All my friends are there. And it's close to my apartment. Besides, no offence, I like your class, but some of the people in it are bitches."

I smile. I've sworn in front of a teacher. What's he going to do? Suspend me?

"I expect you're talking about Mina," Mr. Khan says wryly. "She's got her fair share of challenges outside of school, Jasmine. I'm sure you can empathize."

What's he talking about? This guy knows nothing about my *challenges*.

"You don't know anything about me," I say, my eyes narrowing. I turn to leave.

"I'm sorry if I offended you," Mr. Khan says hastily. "I just remember when your sister disappeared. That's all. It was such a huge media story."

I stop. His words cause my heart to shatter into what feels like a thousand tiny shards of glass inside my chest. Such a huge media story. It's true. That's the sad legacy of my sister's life: another young girl abducted and killed by a sick person. Whenever people hear her name, that's all they think of and that's all they know about her.

"All I'm saying is that sometimes things happen because they're meant to happen. Perhaps you're meant to be at Beaconsfield."

I slowly turn back around and stare at him. Tears threaten to cascade down my cheeks. Is he implying that what happened to Jade was *meant* to happen? I shake my head in disbelief. I want to scream at Mr. Khan, to tell him he has no right to speak about my sister. But, once again, I'm unable to find my voice, and so I turn and I run. And the entire time I'm running, I'm vibrating with rage. I never want to step foot in that stupid school again. Not only do I hate Mina, now I also hate Mr. Khan. I don't stop running until I'm home.

I open the door to our apartment and nearly fall, doubled over, into the front hall. My breath comes in jagged gulps; my lungs are on fire.

"Jasmine?" Mom calls from the kitchen.

The smell of roasting chicken, mingled with onions and garlic, wafts over me. I'm instantly happier, though I'm not sure if it's because of the thought of a delicious dinner or the fact that Mom feels well enough today to even cook.

I straighten up, run my fingers through my hair and vow never to think about that screwed-up school again.

Smile. Breathe. I'll just consider tomorrow the official start of my school year.

I walk into the kitchen. Mom is washing rice in a pot, carefully swirling the water and rinsing it out again. She'll do this until the water is crystal clear. Lola is cutting up tomatoes and onion for a salad.

"Something smells good," I say, putting my arms around Mom and giving her a sideways hug.

"Where's mine?" Lola asks, putting down the knife she's using and wiping at the tears trickling down her cheeks from the onions. She walks over, wraps her tree-trunk-like arms around my shoulders, and hugs me deeply. The smell of shea butter and onion juice engulfs me.

"Thank you for finding my Ibeji doll," she says, giving me a wide smile. "She's very important to me."

"It kind of found me," I mutter as she lets me go. "I'll have to get it for you later. I put it in my room for safe-keeping." There's no way I'm going to touch that thing with bare hands, but I also don't want Lola or Mom coming into my room to get it because of the box. I decide not to tell Lola how her doll nearly caused me to end up hospitalized with a broken neck. Some things are better left unsaid. Instead, I bound over to the oven, open the door, and inhale deeply. My mouth fills with saliva. "Smells amazing."

"Lola's treat," Mom says. She puts the pot on the counter and turns off the water. "Was today any better at school?" she asks, drying her hands on the front of her black pants.

"Nope," I reply. "But it doesn't matter now, anyway." I turn to Lola. "Did you provide this delicious dinner in celebration of the fact that I will finally be going to a school where the students and teachers are sane? You should see the people at Beaconsfield. What a bunch of freaks."

Lola ignores my comment about the school. Instead, she grabs me by the arm and leads me over to the French press Mom uses for her morning cup of chicory.

"Smell this," she says, her eyes dancing with mischief as she lifts the press toward my nose. Deep-brown liquid sloshes inside it. A curl of water vapour escapes from the spout, which means it's a freshly made pot.

I raise an eyebrow at Lola. Has she lost it?

"I know what chicory smells like," I say with a laugh. "You know I hate the stuff. Too bitter."

"This is liquid gold, not chicory," Lola says with a wide smile. "Coffee. The finest Costa Rican beans. A hundred dollars a kilogram."

"What? Where did you manage to get coffee?" I put my nose up to the spout of the press and breathe in deeply. "Mmmm … it smells good. Better than chicory, for sure. I can see why there were so many coffee shops back in the day."

Lola laughs. "Back in the day? Less than fifteen years ago you couldn't go more than a city block without tripping over a Starbucks café. Multi-billion-dollar business."

"I bet schools were better back then as well," I say. "So glad I'm finally starting at Riverdale soon."

Mom frowns. "Jasmine, they still won't let me register you at Riverdale. I spoke to the principal this afternoon. He says your acceptance letter was a mistake."

I stare at her in disbelief. "A m-mistake?" I stutter. Every part of my body suddenly feels cold. This can't be happening.

"Some of the students from your school had to be sent to Beaconsfield because there was not enough space at Riverdale. There are just so many families pouring into the city these days."

"Isn't that the truth," Lola says, nodding her head.

Okay, I know that I should be grateful to even be in school, and to be in one of the few remaining places in the world with an abundance of clean water and more than a trace amount of rainfall. However, I really don't feel like having a discussion about the impact of climate change on the city's population right now. I just want to know that I will be able to get out of that school and away from those weirdos.

"But I haven't seen anyone — and I mean not one single person — that I know at Beaconsfield," I protest. "And, besides, we live around the corner from Riverdale. Kids who live farther away should be going to that idiotic excuse of a school, not me."

Mom shakes her head. "I know," she says. "It doesn't make sense to me either. There must've been some sort of lottery system. I'm going to speak to the superintendent, but can't get in until late next week. That was the first available appointment she had, apparently."

Mom runs a hand through my hair and kisses my cheek. The familiar vanilla scent of her perfume washes over me. "*Pobrecita*, I know it's disappointing, but I just need you to go there until we figure this out."

"Don't worry," Lola says. "I'll go down with your mom if need be. I've got my ways of persuading people." She winks at me. "For what it's worth, I don't think you should be at that school either, my love."

"Thanks," I say. "I guess a few more days there won't kill me."

Mom smiles at me. Her relief at my response is evident. "Such a good attitude. My girl is really growing up," she says to Lola before turning her attention back to the pot of rice.

"I'm just going to put my stuff in my room before dinner," I say, leaving the kitchen.

"Can you get my Ibeji for me?" Lola calls after me. I don't tell her how glad I'll be to return it, and I just hope she won't ask why I'm giving it back wrapped in a t-shirt because there's no way I'm touching it with my bare skin again.

As I walk down the hall, I think about how much I hate lying to Mom. I really do. And I've never pulled anything like what I'm about to, but it's for my own sanity. I know Mom will work things out, and I'll get to Riverdale eventually. But until then, I'm not stepping foot back into that messed-up school.

CHAPTER 5

I'm getting ready to leave the apartment, trying to act as though I'm actually going to school today. My knapsack is on my back, and in it I've got a book about serial killers, my water bottle, and a chicken sandwich (because I know I'm going to get hungry). I also have thirty dollars on my swipe card in case I want to go somewhere or get something to eat or drink. It's going to be a long day.

"See you," I say to Mom, giving her a kiss on the cheek. She's in surprisingly good health today: her eyes are bright and she looks well rested. And, though it could just be my imagination playing tricks on me, I swear she's leaning less on her cane.

"Just a couple of days," she says, kissing me firmly on both cheeks. "Remember that I am so proud of you. Especially the way you're handling all of this. I know it can't be easy."

I instantly feel guilty and nearly change my mind about my plans for the day. But then I remember Mina's insults and Mr. Khan's nosiness, and I steel myself.

The air outside wraps itself around me like a blanket. It's hot, so hot I immediately begin to sweat. Beads of perspiration trickle down my face and back. The wind is as dry as sand and sucks every bit of moisture out of my skin with the efficiency of a vacuum.

It's weird. When I was younger, autumn weather usually brought a chill to the air, and its frosty nights meant warmer clothes. By Halloween it would rarely be sunny and warm. But if it was, Jade and I loved it because it meant we could go trick-or-treating without jackets over our costumes. She always dressed up as something pretty and nice, like a princess or ballerina. I, on the other hand, was usually a goth, a vampire, or — my all-time favourite costume — Edward Scissorhands. He's a character from a really old movie, but it's one of my favourites. And Mom worked really hard making that costume for me. She spent weeks making enormous papier mâché scissors, and then Halloween night she spent over an hour teasing my hair and gelling it just right. She even did my makeup so that it looked identical to Edward's.

That was the last Halloween I ever went trick-or-treating. Jade disappeared a week later.

Now it feels like July in October, and our winters hit in November with ferocious storms and only the slightest dip in temperatures. Instead of blizzards, we get monsoons. They blow across the Atlantic from England due to changes in the jet streams.

At first most people loved the change in the weather, especially here in Toronto when our winters became warmer and there was no longer any snowfall.

Climate-change scientists, however, continued to alert us to the doom ahead.

"Would all of you be smiling and happy if suddenly the sun shone twenty-four hours a day?" I remember one famous environmental scientist shouting during an interview on the evening news. It was a particularly hot evening, at the beginning of the massive power outages. That week there'd been major blackouts across most of North America due to excessive energy consumption. The environmentalists blamed it on all the air-conditioning we were pumping out because of the soaring temperatures. Now blackouts happen all the time because of the constant heat. And there's no longer any real change in seasons. It's as though winter, spring, and autumn have all become extinct, along with 60 percent of the world's species.

I walk about five blocks toward downtown, trying to decide what to do with my day. At first I figure I'll spend most of my time in a park somewhere far away from our neighbourhood, so there's less chance of running into anyone who knows me. But it's so hot I can't stand the thought of being outside a minute more than I have to be.

As I get closer to the downtown area, the shops change from bargain stores and small, family-run vegetable and fruit shops to smart boutiques and trendy chicory cafés. There's less garbage on the streets and in the alleyways and more people wearing suits and looking stressed out and impatient, rather than strung out and sad.

I stop to readjust my knapsack. My T-shirt is soaked through from where the pack was sitting against my back. Gross. Sweat is dripping into my eyes, as well, making them sting uncomfortably. I rub at them, which only makes things worse. That's when I decide to go underground.

I walk toward a set of stairs that leads underneath the sidewalk. At the entrance, sitting just off to the side, is an older woman with badly bleached, tornado-like hair and skin that's so wrinkled it looks like it needs a good ironing. She's sitting on a squashed cardboard box, wearing a red-and-white wool poncho. Just the sight of it makes me want to faint from heat exhaustion.

There's a Styrofoam cup plunked in front of her, but she's just sitting there, staring at her hands, rather than asking people for money. Someone's put an unopened bottle of water down beside her.

I try to leave as much space as possible between me and this lady. Not that I have anything against homeless people or people with mental illness. I'm just afraid she'll smell, and considering the way the heat is making me feel, I don't want to lose my breakfast all over the sidewalk.

"Stop," she says, looking up from her hands and directly at me as I pass.

Great. I always seem to attract the freaks and weirdos. Still, Mom taught me never to be rude to my elders, and I'm sure this woman is treated badly by strangers every single day, so I stop for a moment, making sure I hold my breath as much as possible.

"Pardon?" I say, taking one tiny step backward.

I'm suddenly struck with an intense feeling of déjà vu.

Her eyes are this amazing blue colour that glitter like ocean water. They seem so young and out of place compared to the weathered and wrinkled face framing them. And her gaze is focused and clear. In fact, she doesn't look like a crazy person at all.

"Listen closely," she says, leaning forward. "One of you is not what you seem and will make the ultimate sacrifice."

Yep. This was exactly the kind of thing I expected she might say. I guess I was wrong about her not being crazy. She's certifiable.

"Okay, thanks," I mumble, skirting around her and continuing to the stairs.

"You need to listen to me," she says, her voice rising sharply as I descend the first few steps. "Don't go down there. They're looking for you. The door has been opened."

Even though I know her words are just insane babble, they still cause a sudden chill to snake its way up my spine. And though I can't put my finger on it, there is something very familiar about her.

I tell myself that I'm just being paranoid because of all the weirdness in my life lately, and I continue down the stairs.

The cool thing about Toronto is that there's practically another whole city underneath it. There are hundreds and hundreds of stores, restaurants, hair salons, offices, and chicory shops that exist under the main part of the downtown. They're all connected by underground pathways that go on for kilometres and kilometres. The best thing about it on a day like today is the fact that the whole place is air-conditioned.

And I'm not disappointed. The air here is like a long, cool drink of water. Immediately I feel more energized and awake. I begin to walk, though I'm not sure where to go. I know I can get to the subway from down here, so I decide to get on it and explore a part of the city I've never been to before.

I follow the signs and crowds of people to the subway entrance. Fifteen dollars is just enough to cover my fare both ways. That leaves me with fifteen dollars to get something to eat.

Staring at the subway lines, I try to choose which station will be my destination. I put my finger on the High Park stop. I've been there only once, when Jade was still alive, during a third-grade field trip to study birds, mammals, and insects. It's a massive park with a small lake and loads of trees, so it should be a bit cooler than other places in the city. If the lake hasn't dried up, that is.

I hold my card against the reader and walk through the sliding gates.

Looking around the subway platform at all the people standing beside me, I feel happy. I've got this overwhelming sense of freedom, probably because I'm skipping school while my friends are stuck in math and geography classes. This thought makes me smile.

The train pulls up in a rush of hot air and the doors slide open, allowing passengers to squeeze their way out, past people who are too impatient to wait before trying to force themselves on. This is definitely a busy station.

"Can't ya just wait until we get off?" a woman with a face the colour of a tomato snaps, spittle flying from her lips onto the face of a young man trying to shove his way into the car.

I decide I don't want someone spitting all over my face, so I wait and slide in just as the chimes sound, signalling the doors are about to close.

Now for the fun part: finding a seat beside someone who a) won't talk nonstop to me; b) doesn't stink and/or isn't eating something that stinks; c) isn't doing something decidedly unhygienic, like picking his nose or cutting his nails; and last, but not least, d) isn't muttering to herself while shooting looks of death toward other passengers.

After some careful searching, I decide to take a seat beside a middle-aged woman reading a romance novel. Books are a pretty rare sight these days. I figure since I've got one of my own in my bag, it might be a sign that she's a safe choice.

I sit down and glance up at the subway map, which is posted above the doors. Only a few stations before I have to change to a westbound train.

I take out my book and open it to the chapter on Myra Hindley. In the 1960s, she and her lover, Ian Brady, kidnapped and murdered several children and teenagers in England. I stare hard at the photo of her, studying her eyes. Since Jade was taken, I've read hundreds of books and newspaper articles about serial killers, especially ones that took children. And the first thing I always do is look at their photos. I want to see if their eyes hold any clues about what kind of person can do such terrible things.

The lights of the subway car flicker on and off a couple of times. A few passengers around me suck in their breath in anticipation. None of us wants to get stuck down here during a power outage.

Blackouts underground often mean evacuations — walking out along the tracks with transit police leading the way. If you're in the wrong spot when the power comes back on, bad luck for you, because it can mean instant electrocution.

Suddenly, the train jolts sickeningly to the right. This time a few people scream. I might be among them.

And that's when everything falls apart.

CHAPTER 6

The same thunderclap I heard when I touched the Ibeji booms through the subway car. My body goes all jiggy as that electrical feeling surges through me again. Except this time I feel a sense of power from it, like I'm a super-hero changing form.

Both my knapsack and book fall from my lap onto the floor. As I bend to retrieve them, I notice some-thing. The woman's legs beside me have changed. Swear to God, she was wearing white linen pants two seconds ago. Now she's actually got some sort of tan-coloured makeup smeared all over her legs, and they're bare. To top it all off, it looks like she's taken eyebrow pencil and drawn a line up the back of them.

The train lurches once more, this time sharply to the left. My knapsack skitters across the floor like a cock-roach, and I notice something that causes me to jam my hand against my mouth to keep from screaming in real terror. That something is the floor of the subway car. It's changed. It's now made of wood. Subway cars in Toronto do not have wooden floors. This much I know for sure.

Before I can think about it a second longer, we're plunged into darkness again. I pull my knees to my chest and close my eyes, wishing for all of this to go away. If this is what going crazy is all about, I want no part of it. It's terrifying. What if I'm still on a normal subway train in Toronto, sitting with my knees up to my chest, whimpering like a terrified puppy? Everyone must be looking, except I wouldn't know it because I'm clearly delusional.

Then the singing begins. At first I can only hear it faintly, but it slowly grows louder. The song isn't familiar, but the people singing it sound happy and energetic.

> Roll out the barrel,
> We'll have a barrel of fun!
> Roll out the barrel,
> We've got the blues on the run!

Gathering every bit of courage I can, I open one eye and then the other.

The lights are back on. But I'm no longer on the train. I'm on a subway platform. The woman with the book is also gone; a different woman sits beside me. She glances over and shoots me a reassuring smile. She's wearing bright red lipstick, and her hair looks the way Mom's great-grandmother's hair does in old photos. And she's pretty dressed up considering we're all sitting on the floor.

I look around. There are actually hundreds of people down here, and more are arriving by the minute. Most have blankets and pillows with them. Some of the kids have stuffed bears. The singing is coming from a group of men and women standing at the other end of the platform. One of the men is playing an accordion. He's wearing an old-fashioned suit and sports a funny moustache that curls up at the edges.

"You all right, love? Do the air raid sirens scare you?" the woman asks. She has an English accent.

I shake my head. It doesn't really matter what I say because clearly this is some sort of psychotic episode. God only knows what I'm doing back in real-time on the subway. Maybe I'm screaming my head off like a lunatic. I imagine this is what Alice in Wonderland must've felt like on the wrong side of the looking glass. But then she's not real either.

Suddenly sirens begin to wail from somewhere above. People try to carry on talking and singing, but the air thickens with an undercurrent of fear.

"Are your parents with you?" the woman asks. Her face is creased with concern. I stop myself from reaching out to touch her, to see if she's solid or just some apparition I've conjured up.

"No," I answer. "My mom is at home."

The concern on the woman's face grows. "Is she on her way here? I suspect those Gerries are really going to give us a pounding tonight."

What is she talking about? I nod, trying to seem as if I have some clue as to what's happening. But I don't. Everyone is dressed funny, and something pretty strange must be going on to make all these people gather below ground.

I glance around. There's a poster on the wall showing a fierce-looking lion in front of the British flag. The words *The Spirit of 1943* are printed below the lion in large, red letters. Beside it is another poster of an old, round, and mostly bald man. He looks a bit like a serious Santa, minus the beard and red hat. The poster of this man is emblazoned with the words *Keep Calm and Carry On*.

"Do you have your gas mask with you?" The woman's still looking at me.

"Gas mask?"

Her brows furrow. "Are you sure you're feeling well?" she says. "I'm asking if you have your issued gas mask. Don't the schools remind you to keep it with you at all times? Remember, Hitler won't give a warning."

I pause and try to decide whether or not to ask this woman where I am and what year it is. Could I have stumbled onto a movie set? There are always loads of films being shot in Toronto, and sometimes they're historical with costumes and old cars and stuff. Maybe this is a movie set, and she's just trying really hard to stay in character.

Then I remember who the man in the poster is. Winston Churchill. My grade eight teacher pointed out his statue last year when we were on a field trip to city hall. He was the British prime minister during the Second World War.

But that was nearly a century ago....

"I need to ask you a strange question," I say.

"Yes?"

"What day is it? I mean, what is the date exactly?"

She looks worried again. That makes two of us.

"Did you hit your head coming here?" she asks. "Perhaps in the last few days? There's so much debris around and loose bits from the bombings."

"No," I reply. Though I'm not really sure. Maybe that's why all of this is happening. Could I be in a coma or something?

"It's Wednesday, March 3," she says.

"But what year is it?" I ask. My bladder feels uncomfortably full, and it's not because I need to urinate. It's a reaction to the fear that is flooding every cell of my body.

"I really think you need to see a medic," the woman says. "You're clearly not well. There's one here, you know."

I shake my head. "Please, I just need you to tell me what year it is."

The woman presses her lips together and nods. It's clear from the look on her face that she thinks I'm crazy. She's not alone.

"Why, it's 1943, of course," she says.

CHAPTER 7

At least her answer makes some sense. And if this is a dream, I give myself brownie points for being so clever: the poster of Winston Churchill, the mention of Hitler, all of us sitting here, crammed together underground like a bunch of canned sardines. Not only can I recall historical details, I can recreate them in my dreams. My old history teacher, Mr. Carter, can stick his mark of 60 percent.

Except now I'm wondering if this isn't a dream. Everything is feeling far too real.

"Of course it's 1943," I say to the woman, with a laugh. "I'm just joking around with you." I smooth down the front of my skirt. Skirt? Yep, I seem to be wearing a tweedy skirt of some sort. It's making my legs itch like crazy. Don't remember ever being itchy in a dream before.

"I don't regard that sort of thing as *funny*, young lady," the woman replies. She looks angry with me. "You need to watch what you say and do. Careless talk helps the Gerries."

"Sorry," I say. "I'll try to remember that. Actually, I think my mother should be arriving any minute."

"Really?" the woman says, a relieved smile flashing across her face. "Perhaps you should move closer to the bottom of the stairwell so she sees you. Just don't get in people's way, mind."

I nod and hoist myself up. My knees feel stiff, as though I've been sitting for a while. As soon as I'm standing, I can see where the stairwell is. A steady stream of people file along the platform from that end.

I decide to head over there, go up the stairs, and see what's at the top. If I come out in Toronto and find a bunch of drone cameras and the white trailers that accompany movie shoots, then I've clearly got some sort of weird amnesia going on and have accidentally stumbled onto a movie set.

But if I get up there and step out into the fog and damp air of London in 1943, well, then I've really lost it.

"Bye," I say to the woman, giving her a half-hearted wave just to be polite. I figure teenagers back in the 1940s were likely way more polite than we are today.

She gives me a tight smile back. Her red lipstick is cracked and flaking in places. I can tell she's relieved to see me go.

I walk as fast as I can toward the people entering the lower part of the station. A lot of them are soaking wet. Their clothing sticks to their bodies like plastic wrap. It must be pouring rain outside, which makes me think I just might find that I'm in London. It hasn't rained in Toronto in more than two months, and according to every weather forecast I've heard lately, that isn't about to change anytime soon. We're officially in the middle of a heat wave, with no precipitation in sight.

It's hard to get anywhere because I'm moving against the crowd. I pass crying children, wide-eyed with fear, wet hair plastered to their faces in spaghetti-like strands. Clear snot runs from their noses to their lips.

Eventually I squeeze myself past everyone and reach the bottom of the stairs. It's pretty dark in the stairwell, and the descending figures are shadowy. Placing my hand on the railing, I begin to slowly work my way up, trying to press myself thin against the wall. The air is damp and the stairs are slippery. I have no idea what kind of footwear I have on, but I do know I'm no longer wearing my Converse sneakers from this morning.

I'm halfway up the stairs when I see her. As she passes me, we turn and look each other directly in the eye.

Even though I can't see her very well, I stop dead in my tracks. The resemblance is uncanny; it's like having a mirror held up to my face. Except the girl in front of me (who has also stopped and is staring back at me) has a tiny birthmark on her right cheekbone … just like Jade.

Her mouth drops open with surprise, and tears well up in her eyes. We're both speechless.

Jade is here! Now I know for sure I've either lost my mind or am having the most realistic dream of my life. Even if I'm dreaming, I'm going to take advantage of every second with her.

I reach out to hug her just as a deafening boom shakes the staircase. Then, from somewhere directly above us, there's the sound of screaming followed by a sickening thud. Within a few seconds there's more screaming. As bodies come hurtling toward us like dominoes, I realize that people are falling over one another and down the slippery steps.

"Jasmine!" Jade cries as she is knocked over by a woman clutching a toddler in her hands. The little girl is torn from her mother's grasp. Jade reaches for me, and I grab her hand, throwing me off-balance. My feet slip out from under me, and now I'm falling as well, bashing my head against the steel railing as I tumble.

I bounce against the edge of one of the steps. Pain shoots up my spine like lightning. My back feels broken and I can't breathe. Panic sweeps over me. I'm still close to the railing, so I reach up and somehow pull myself halfway to standing. At least I can breathe again. I wipe my mouth and stare at the splotch of fresh blood on the back of my hand. My lip is bleeding heavily.

Jade is somewhere in this crush of people. I need to find her. Panic claws at my chest like a wild animal. I try to lift an elderly lady, who's softly moaning, but she keeps sliding from my clutch as though she's made of silly putty. She's also as cold as ice. If it weren't for her moaning, I'd think she was dead for sure.

No one can be this cold and still be alive. I guess it's all part of the dream. Tears blur my vision. Jade. I've got to get to Jade. People are moaning and crying all around me. This has turned into the worst nightmare I've ever had, and I want it to end. Now.

Suddenly, strong arms circle my waist, pulling me up and away from the pile of bodies. I'm being carried along the very top of the railing, even though I know it's impossible. Even a circus performer with the best balance in the world couldn't pull this off, which means I just might be dreaming after all.

Adrenaline floods my body as I realize I'm being taken away from Jade. She's probably hurt and suffocating under the crush of bodies on the stairwell.

"Stop!" I shout, trying to twist my body out of my rescuer's grasp. "Let me go!"

There's no response from whoever has me, so I try to pry the slender fingers off my waist. The air is getting colder and clearer. We're reaching the entrance to the subway station.

I begin to sob and tear desperately at the hands holding me. Though I realize this person has likely just saved my life, Jade is still down there. I can't leave her. I don't want her to be alone again. Even if this is just a dream. I can't abandon her again.

My feet touch solid ground. Rain lashes at my face. As the hold on me relaxes, I spin around to confront my rescuer.

CHAPTER 8

"I need you to listen closely to me, Jasmine," Raphael says.

The shock of coming face-to-face with him renders me speechless. But after a few seconds of silence, I begin to laugh. It's a crazy cackle. I throw my head back for effect. I'm starting to get pretty good at this whole insanity thing.

"Okay," I say, poking his chest with my finger. He's solid. I throw him a lopsided grin that I hope is both flirtatious and confident. "I know you. You're the cute boy from Beaconsfield. I thought I might dream about you eventually. So now that we've cleared that up, I need to go back down there."

I spin around, but Raphael grabs my arm before I can even take a step.

"We don't have a lot of time," he says impatiently. "I can't explain everything to you right now, but I need to get you away from here. Fast."

I laugh again. "Right. Because *they're* looking for me." I snap my fingers close to Raphael's face. He doesn't flinch. "Just like the crazy lady said."

His eyes narrow. "We'll talk about this disrespect for your Protectors later," he says.

I come closer to his face. "Why don't you be my protector, big boy?" I say, leaning in to kiss him.

He pushes me away, panic flashing across his face. Good. It's nice to see that the boy is actually able to show emotion.

The rain is coming down harder now. I hear loud booming sounds, like the approach of a violent thunderstorm, off in the distance.

"You're being an idiot," I snap, pushing my wet hair off my face. "I'm going back down to get my sister. Even if she's a figment of my imagination, I'm going back for her."

Raphael grabs my arm again. This time his hold is much firmer. "You have no idea what you can do," he says.

I struggle against his grip. I need to get to Jade. For a brief second, I consider biting him to get him to release me.

"Right now I need you to stop being angry and do what I say. I have to get you to a safer place. You can't go back down there."

I stop for a moment. It's night time. If I choose to believe I'm not dreaming, then London sits in front of me in the pitch darkness. I've never been to England, let alone London, but I do know that it is a huge city. And, dream or not, I seem to be in the middle of a blackout during a Second World War air raid.

"But my twin sister is there. I can't just leave her to die." The absurdity of my words strikes me; I've already left her once before, and she is dead. Suffocation on a stairwell in my dream is a far better way to go than what likely happened to her in real life. I'm pretty aware of the fact that abducted children are generally abused before being murdered and then discarded like yesterday's trash.

"As long as they don't get to you, Jade will be kept alive," Raphael replies. "You need to get over this guilt. It's preventing you from seeing what is really happening. They need both of you together, and right now you're being far too reckless. You're feeding into them."

"Who is this 'they' you keep talking about?" I ask.

Raphael ignores my question and turns.

I follow him as he walks away, and we stumble through the darkness together.

The air is damp and cold. I'm only wearing a blouse and a sweater vest, and I'm shivering uncontrollably.

"How can you walk so fast?" I ask. I can barely see my hand in front of my face it's so dark.

"I know this city well," Raphael replies. "We're going to Whitechapel Station."

"To meet Jack the Ripper?" I ask in mock terror.

An exasperated sigh cuts through the air. "I'm glad you find this amusing," he says. "I'm taking you there so we can get you back through."

"Through?" I ask. What the hell is he talking about? I stub my toe against something that feels like a pile of broken bricks. Pain shoots through my foot. "Ow!" Tears spring to my eyes.

"Be careful. There's loads of debris all over," Raphael says. "This part of the city gets hit really hard by the bombings because of the docklands."

"Okay," I say. "Can you at least answer one question? Can you tell me how is it that I'm here in *London* in *1943* with *you*, when we actually live in *Toronto* in *2030*? And while you're at it, please explain how Jade, my dead sister, is here, too. But you're telling me she's alive. Clearly, this is some sort of crazy dream. Did I have a seizure or something on the subway in Toronto?"

"Was Jade's body ever found?" Raphael asks, his voice quiet.

"What do you mean?" Defensiveness rises in me like a tidal wave.

"Keep your voice down and stop being angry. It's not helping you," Raphael cautions. "I'm asking you to think about her disappearance. Was she ever found?"

"No." I answer. My mind races back to that horrible year. It wasn't long after our tenth birthday. Mom cried constantly. Lola stayed with us the entire time, feeding and taking care of us, even though her own son, Femi, was seriously ill with leukemia.

There were police and volunteer searches almost daily. Lola would go and help comb the nearby ravines and city parks, then come back and care for Mom, Femi, and I.

Eventually, Lola was able to pay for special cancer treatment in the United States for Femi, and he was cured. Mom and I weren't as lucky. No amount of money could bring Jade back to us.

The police were at a loss about her disappearance. They didn't have any viable leads. Strange vans, people who'd been behaving oddly in the neighbourhood — all the tips given by the public turned into dead ends. Jade had seemingly vanished into thin air.

Only I knew the truth. I'd been there when the tall boy with the spiky, black hair approached us. I didn't recognize him. He wasn't one of the high school kids who walked by our house every day. After the disappearance, once his description garnered no leads, everyone chocked my story about him up to shock, as another way I was trying to cope with everything. Eventually, I began to doubt his existence, too.

Jade and I were sprawled on the front lawn. I was reading a book, and Jade was drawing in her sketchbook. When the boy's shadow fell across the grass, my blood turned to ice. I started shivering. I remember feeling confused, because the day was quite warm and sunny.

"Girls, I've lost my kitten," he said, showing us a glossy photo. "She's really young, and ran out my front door." There was a strange flatness in his voice. The fluffy, white-haired, blue-eyed kitten in his photograph looked exactly like the ones from the toilet paper commercials. Jade and I loved those kittens. They were exactly the type we wanted as a pet.

That was when I reached out and touched the photo, and for a split second, everything tilted as if the world had been knocked off its axis. I looked up, and the boy and I locked eyes. Fear rose in my throat like vomit. Whimpering, I got up and began pulling at Jade's arm.

His eyes were dead. They were as black as the deepest ocean and lifeless, like the eyes of the fish I'd see lying limply over piles of ice in Kensington Market on Saturdays when Mom took us shopping. His bloodless lips pulled back into a smirk, and that's when my bladder gave out. Warm urine ran down the length of my legs.

But Jade continued smiling at the boy. "We need to help him, Jasmine," she said. "The kitten could be hurt."

"Look at him!" I screamed.

And that's when he tried to grab me. I turned and ran as fast as my legs could carry me toward the front door of our house. I needed to get Mom so she could help us. I burst through the front door and into the kitchen where she was drinking coffee and reading the newspaper at the table.

By the time we got outside, both Jade and the boy with the dead eyes were gone.

I should never have left her.

CHAPTER 9

We reach Whitechapel Station after about twenty minutes of me stumbling over a variety of rubble and unknown obstacles, nearly breaking my neck while Raphael somehow continued to walk like a cat in the complete darkness.

When we get to the top of the stairs, he turns to me and leans in close. "This is going to be a bit dangerous for you, Jazz," he says in a voice that reminds me of the stage whispers we practise in drama class. "They've somehow managed to get you here, and now they'll do anything to keep you … at least until they can kill you. You and Jade."

I lick a raindrop off my upper lip and stare at him. "Aren't you going to tell me who 'they' are?"

"If you keep your mind clear, you'll know," he replies in that frustratingly vague way of his. "You'll be able to see them for what they really are."

"Will they be wearing polka-dotted Converse?" I ask.

"When you were young, you could see them," he says, ignoring my quip. "Remember the one that took Jade?"

My body turns to ice. "How do you know about that?" I snap. "What are you, some sort of freak? I mean, how do you even know my sister's name?"

"I'll tell you everything as soon as we are out of here. All I can say right now is that when you see them, you'll recognize them. But — and this is really important, Jazz — you can't let them know that you realize what they are."

"Okay," I say. "So what are '*they*'? Seriously, I need an answer."

"Demons," Raphael replies. "Demons and lost souls inhabit this place. We're in the Place-in-Between."

Okay. Maybe I'm not the only crazy one here....

"Demons?" I ask skeptically. "Lost souls? The Place-in-Between? In between what? I was on my way to High Park, so that would make this ... Parkdale, right?"

Raphael frowns at me. "I'll explain later. We need to get moving. They know you're here."

"I won't go down there unless I know more," I insist. "Think about it — you're telling me there are gangs of demons underground that want to get a hold of me to kill me, and you expect me to just follow you like some stupid puppy dog?"

There's that exasperated sigh again. He runs a hand through his hair. I'm really irritating him now.

"Okay. In short, there is a place between the human world and the underworld where souls who are confused or have unresolved issues from their mortal lives end up. Some humans call this place Limbo. We call it the Place-in-Between. The main gateway to it is directly under a city humans chose to mark the beginning of time; a city where countless tragedies have occurred over thousands of years."

"The beginning of time?" I pause for a moment. "The Meridian Line in Greenwich? London's above the gateway?"

He nods. "Several times throughout human history, there have been periods of extraordinary demon activity. These were times when the darker spirits were able to feed off humankind's collective negative emotions and become very strong. During those times they were strong enough to take human form, walk the Earth, and influence events."

"You're speaking like a fifty-nine-year-old professor," I say.

"I really can't believe you're a Seer, let alone ..." he stops speaking and shakes his head. "You're bloody impossible. Let's go. We're running out of time."

He grabs my right arm and begins to guide me down the stairs, keeping me close beside him. "You need to focus on Toronto the way you left it. It's still there in time and space. Visualize it in your mind when we get down there, Jazz. That's how you can get back. Hold on to that image, no matter what. And remember, the demons can't hurt you unless you believe they can."

"And if I believe they can?" I ask.

He grimaces. "Just keep your wits about you and your fear suppressed. Negative emotions make the demons' energy stronger, and there's already a great amount of fear and despair being expressed by the souls that are trapped here."

I stop and look at him. "Does this mean that Jade is stuck in the Place-in-Between? Is she a lost soul?" Tears blur my vision.

He doesn't answer me for a moment.

"Well?" I ask.

"I don't know everything, Jazz. What I do know is that you're much more powerful than an average human...."

"But?" I ask. It's clear he's holding back. He knows more than he's willing to admit.

"But not as powerful as you'd be with Jade," he finishes.

"Then we need to find her, right?" I ask. "If being together will help protect me ... us."

"Unfortunately, being together down here also makes you more vulnerable. I'm not sure how or why she ended up in this place. But I do know I need to get you away from here as soon as possible."

"What's happening to me?" I ask him. "Am I going crazy? Is that why I'm imagining all of these messed-up things?"

We continue down the staircase.

"Absolutely not," Raphael replies. "You're very sane. But you're going to need to hold on to that sanity as tightly as possible in the near future."

"And just how near is the near future?"

He looks at me. "Right now."

We've reached the main platform of the station. There are loads of people jammed into this subway station as well. They're huddled under blankets on the tracks and along the entire length of the platform — just about anywhere there's a bit of space to stretch out. Some people are playing cards; some are sleeping restlessly. It smells of body odour, bad breath, and stale farts. Other than the fact that we're all hiding from Nazi bombs in Limbo, it seems like one gigantic sleepover.

A woman walks toward us, close enough for me to smell the sweet perfume she's wearing. The scent reminds me of dying flowers. I turn my head to watch her pass. She's quite glamorous, reminding me of an old-fashioned movie star, like Michelle Pfeiffer. She's wearing a dress the colour of robins' eggs. A matching, tiny pillbox hat is perched atop her wavy, red hair.

Suddenly, she stops, turns back, and looks right at me. Her gaze is so intense, it makes me feel naked. I give her a half-hearted smile, thinking maybe I annoyed her by staring. Then I notice her eyes: flat, dark, and very cold. I can't see any pupils. They're like the eyes of a shark I once saw in a documentary … and the eyes of the boy that took Jade away. Demon's eyes. Raphael's right: I have seen this creature before. The crazy thing is, it looks so human it almost blends in seamlessly with everyone else down here.

Raphael takes my hand. It's as if he's also seen her, though that's impossible because he's on the other side of me, staring straight ahead.

Then the smell and cold hit me. It's like I've just stepped into a fridge full of fresh blood. That's what the smell is. It's the smell of butcher shops. And death. I begin to shake uncontrollably and my bladder loosens. Raphael gives my hand a firm squeeze.

His words echo in my mind: *They can't hurt you unless you believe they can.*

I close my eyes for a moment and try to visualize Toronto and the subway car I was sitting in. I think about how the blue-and-red fabric of the seat felt rough against my legs when I first sat down, how the man across from me kept rhythmically tapping a pen against the metal pole in front of him, oblivious to the dirty looks he was getting from everyone around him. I want to be back there so badly.

I open my eyes again. It's still 1943, and I'm still in a subway tunnel in jolly old Limbo-England. Great.

"Remember, it can't hurt you unless you grant it the power to," Raphael whispers, leaning in close. His breath on my ear sends shivers up my spine.

"Stop being afraid, Jazz. It feeds on fear. And if you become too afraid, it will be hard to leave here."

I take a deep breath, look the woman, or whatever it is, in the eye, and smile.

"Do I know you?" I ask.

CHAPTER 10

In response to my question, the thing draws its lips back into a half-smile, half-snarl, revealing incredibly straight, sharp teeth, lined up in rows like soldiers ready to attack. A moment later the face changes. Like a kaleidoscope, it morphs from being human into a pointy-nosed, fox-like face without fur.

It looks just like the thing that took Jade.

That's when I scream. I can't help it. My screaming sets off a chain reaction; several of the children and adults around me begin to scream in unison.

"Run!" Raphael shouts.

In the split second it takes my brain to send the signal to my body that we've got to get out of here, the thing reaches for me. Its claws bite into the fleshy part of my upper arm, tearing the fabric of my shirt as my legs propel me forward.

"Don't look back," Raphael says. Though we are running as fast as possible, he doesn't seem out of breath at all, meanwhile I can't even manage to find enough oxygen to even reply. I figure he doesn't expect me to anyhow. And he needn't worry about me slowing down; there's no way I'm going to turn back to have a look at the monster pursuing us.

We scramble down to track level, weaving our way in and around the people that are bedding down for the night. I wonder if these are souls that died during the war or ones that simply ended up stuck down here in Limbo and now have to experience the terror of the Blitz eternally. If that's the case, do they remember their former lives? Or does being down here somehow make them forget?

Jade remembered, though. She called out to me, called my name, just as everyone began to tumble down the stairwell.

Raphael leads us deeper into the darkness of the subway tunnel. Here only a few candles flicker and it's much, much colder. Dampness envelops me like a glove. There aren't nearly as many people taking shelter this far into the tunnel, and the ones that are can't be clearly seen. Bodies line the tunnel walls, shrouded by blankets. The light from the candles creates shadows that dance across their faces as we race by. It's impossible to tell if they are male or female, young or old. I imagine this is what a morgue must be like.

I'm not supposed to be here, I think. *This is a place for the dead.*

Something grabs at me from under a blanket as I sprint by. I see the movement out of the corner of my eye, but it's too late. Cold fingers latch onto my right ankle. Their hold is strong. My hand is wrenched from Raphael's, and I cry out for him as I tumble down into the darkness.

"Think about Toronto," Raphael shouts. "Visualize it in your mind!"

Tiny bursts of fireworks dance in front of my eyes as the side of my head smashes against the cold metal of the tracks.

The last thing I feel is a sharp pain reverberating through my skull before everything goes black and silent.

Cold. It's so cold. I roll over onto my back, which sends bolts of sharp pain skipping across my brain. Someone's groaning. It takes a couple of seconds before I realize the person groaning is me.

"It's okay, Jazz."

The voice is familiar. I open one eye, then the other, squinting against the bright light. Everything hurts. Above me, Raphael is barely recognizable. His face floats above mine like an angel's. Though he's coming in and out of focus, he's gorgeous as usual. I smile through the pain.

"Where am I?" My voice sounds tiny and far away.

"Here's some water for her," a woman says. I open my eyes a bit wider. The woman, who looks to be in her early thirties, hands Raphael a bottle of water. She's wearing loose-fitting jeans, a pair of fashionably scuffed motorcycle boots, and a black tank top. It's definitely not a 1940s wartime outfit.

"You're in the subway, of course," Raphael says, twisting the clear plastic cap off the water bottle. He cups the back of my head gently, helps me sit up, and guides the bottle to my lips.

"You fainted and hit your head," the woman says. She bends down and takes my hand. I stare at her incredibly long lashes. They nearly graze her cheekbones when she blinks.

"What? What station am I in?" I stammer.

"Bay Station," Raphael replies. He nods at the woman. "Thanks so much for helping out. I'll make sure she gets home. We live in the same apartment building."

My eyes widen. We do? That's news to me.

"Okay, then," the woman says, straightening up. She shoots me a sympathetic smile. "Hope you feel better."

I try to smile back at her, but it's hard. My body feels like it has just come out on the losing end of a battle with a wild animal. Could fainting make me feel this terrible?

"Are you sure this is Bay Station?" I ask, propping myself up onto my elbows. Vertigo sweeps over me. I steady myself. "What happened to London? And that thing that was chasing me?"

"I have no idea what you're talking about, Jazz."

I'm fully sitting up now, watching people pass us. This is definitely Toronto. And, considering the amount of people hurrying by, it appears to be the beginning of rush hour. How long was I unconscious? I feel the back of my head. Ouch. The skin is tender and sensitive to my touch. There's a massive goose egg forming back there.

Raphael frowns. "Maybe we should taxi over to the hospital to make sure you don't have a concussion."

I slowly haul myself to my feet. "How is it that you keep appearing wherever I am?"

Raphael stares at me, his expression blank. "What do you mean?"

I narrow my eyes at him. "Don't pretend you have no idea what I'm talking about. It's effing creepy. Are you following me? If everything is so normal, then why aren't you in class? Why are you here?"

"It's four o'clock, Jasmine," he replies. "School is over. May I ask why you weren't there today?"

It's four o'clock? It was only ten when I got on the subway. How could six hours have passed? I was counting on getting home before Mom got back from the hospital, so I could erase any messages from the school about me being absent.

"Like you don't know where I was," I retort, brushing off the front of my jeans.

Raphael shakes his head. "Why would I ask you if I knew?"

"Then it's none of your business," I say, throwing my backpack over my shoulder. My muscles ache every time I move, but I'm not about to let him know that. "And I can find my own way home. Thanks."

I turn and begin to walk. Every time my foot hits the ground, a thudding pain echoes through my head. I have no idea what happened to me today, but my gut feeling is that it was a whole lot more than a simple case of fainting. Raphael being here proves that. And if he's going to act like a complete twat and pretend everything is normal, he can screw off.

"Wait," he says, falling into step beside me.

I ignore him and move onto the escalator. It's definitely rush hour; escalators aren't run at other times anymore. It's another way to conserve energy.

He grabs onto my arm and leans in close. "It's not safe to talk about things here," he whispers. I involuntarily shiver again. He really needs to stop doing this whisper-in-the-ear thing. It's driving me crazy.

I turn and look directly at him. "Are you saying what I think you're saying?"

He glances around. No one on the escalator seems to be paying attention to our discussion. They've all got these stressed-out, unhappy-commuter expressions on their faces.

"The gateway somehow opened and dragged you into a place you shouldn't have been," he whispers. "And I don't know if that means the gateway is allowing *them* into this world again, as well. But either way, we can't take any chances until we know more."

"So it wasn't all a dream?" I ask, keeping my voice low. "I mean, London and those … creatures? Jade?"

Raphael gazes at me solemnly. "It definitely wasn't a dream."

CHAPTER 11

It seems that Raphael does live in my building after all. We walk back from the station because I'm not taking public transportation again until I know how it sucked me away and spat me out in Limbo.

"How long have you lived here?" I ask as he touches his thumb against the security pad on the building's entry system.

"A little under a month."

"Strange that I've never seen you," I say. "But then strange seems to be the major theme in my life these days, so I'm not surprised."

We walk into the front lobby. As usual it smells ripe. The stench of the day appears to be *eau de body odour* mingled with stale cigarette smoke. Lovely. Mr. Jones, one of the more notorious elderly tenants, is sitting in the corner, his one-eyed mop of a dog lying at his feet. Though the dog might've begun life white, its bathless existence has resulted in a fur coat that is permanently a gross, dirty-dishwater grey.

"Hi, Mr. Jones," I say, plastering a smile onto my face.

He grunts at me, fumbles around in the pocket of his sweat-stained, plaid shirt, and produces a half-smoked cigarette. Shaking like a spider in a snowstorm, he wedges the cigarette between his thin lips and expertly ignites it with a plastic lighter.

"Good afternoon, Mr. Jones," Raphael says.

"Hello, Raphael," Mr. Jones answers. "What's shakin'?"

"Everything's well, thank you. What did your vet say about Toffee?" Raphael asks, walking over. I stare in disgust as he bends down to pet the dog. There's no way I'd be touching that thing gloveless.

Then Mr. Jones does something I've never seen him do in all the years I've lived here. He smiles. His stubby teeth are nicotine yellow, and more than a few are missing, but it's definitely a smile. All he's ever done with me is grunt and stare, like I'm something nasty stuck on the bottom of his shoe.

"Jus' like you said," Mr. Jones replies. "The tumour is all gone. Went in expectin' the euthanasia and walked out with a clean bill of health for 'im." He smiles again, sucks deeply on his cigarette, and then bends to pet the dog. "Don't understand it, but can't thank you and your brother enough for getting us that appointment."

"Not a worry," Raphael says. "We love animals, and Mike didn't want to see you unable to take care of Toffee because of vet bills. Don't forget to bring him around on Sunday, so we can give him a grooming. Consider it a celebratory bath."

Mr. Jones laughs. It's a hoarse laugh, betraying years of cigarette smoking. "Did you hear that, Toffee?" he says, leaning down close to the mop of grey fur. "Not only do you get a new lease on life, but a good scrubbing, too!"

"See you Sunday, then? We'll come by and pick her up for you," Raphael says, with a wave goodbye before turning back to me. We walk away, leaving Mr. Jones happily sucking on his cigarette.

I punch the elevator button, and then step inside as the doors slide open. I'm relieved it's actually working for once; the way I'm feeling, the stairs would've been torture.

"What's up with you and Mr. Jones?" I ask as soon as we're out of earshot. "The only thing in the world that cranky man cares about is his smelly dog."

Raphael leans against the wall of the elevator. "Actually, that's not true. What is true is that that dog is the only living creature to show unconditional love to Harvey for as long as he can remember."

"Harvey?" I snort. "You're on a first-name basis?"

Raphael raises an eyebrow at me. "If you would only pay closer attention, you'd know all these things for yourself. You've built up so many defences since Jade disappeared. And now, with everything that's happening, those defences are proving dangerous."

"You keep giving me mysterious lectures," I say as we step out of the elevator and into the shadowy light of the hallway. "Can't you tell me more than just to think clearly and not be negative?"

"I can tell you more, but there are some things I can't explain right now."

I open the front pocket of my knapsack and pull out my house keys. "Is my apartment safe enough to talk about things?" I ask.

Raphael nods. "I believe so."

As soon as we walk into the apartment, I'm floored by the smell of cleaning products and the spotlessness of the front hall. Though I try to keep things as tidy as possible, sometimes with the help of Lola, it's been a losing battle against dust and clutter for a few years now, ever since Mom got really sick. But walking in today you wouldn't know it: everything is orderly and sparkling. The scent of lemons and bleach fills the air. I wonder if Lola hired a cleaning lady for the day.

I hang my knapsack on the coat rack. It feels wrong to just drop it on the floor the way I usually do.

The second thing that shocks me is that Mom *walks* out to greet us. And she's not using her cane. In fact, her limp isn't even noticeable.

"What a nice surprise," she says. "It's Raphael, right?"

My mouth drops open. "You know each other?"

"Raphael and his brother helped me after my treatment the other day," Mom says, motioning us into the living room. "I wasn't feeling well, so they helped me inside and to get comfortable. It was the day Lola had to leave early because of work. Let me grab us something to drink. So hot out there, no?"

"Yeah, it's boiling out," I say. "Let me get the drinks, though."

Mom waves me away, as if I'm an annoying fly. "Don't be silly. I'll make some fresh lemonade." She turns to go to the kitchen.

"Wait, Mom," I say. I pause, biting my lower lip. "Um, did anyone call today?"

She stops and turns to me. "Other than a hundred charities trying to raise money for all the victims of drought? No. Why? Are you expecting a call?"

I shrug. "I just thought Savitri was going to call me about this media project she wants help with."

"No, Savitri didn't call. Wouldn't she have called your phone?"

"I let the battery run down," I say. Lie number three of the day to Mom. However, I've got to admit, I feel more relieved about her not finding out about me skipping school than guilty about my dishonesty.

She leaves Raphael and me standing awkwardly in the middle of the room, staring at each other.

"Mind if I sit down?" he asks.

I've completely forgotten to be polite. Mom would have my head.

"Sorry," I say as I sit down on the velvet chair. "Make yourself comfortable." I motion toward the sofa. It's the only other place to sit in the room.

Raphael takes a seat and then leans toward me. "I'll explain as much as I can, but will need to stop when your mom comes," he says. "She knows nothing about this. About what you and Jade are."

"Okay," I say with a nod. My heart swells with hope hearing Jade being spoken about in the present tense.

"You have to be at Beaconsfield because there are people looking out for you there. Protecting you. They look out for all the Seers."

"You mentioned that word before," I say. "When we were in … London." The words sound crazy as soon as they're out of my mouth. "What's a Seer?"

"I'll tell you in a moment. But first, did you notice anything odd about the school? About Beaconsfield?"

"Are you joking? Where do you want me to start? It's practically a circus freak show."

He does that exasperated sigh again. "A yes would suffice, Jazz. For instance, did you notice that there are a significant number of female twins there?"

"I'd have to be a complete idiot to not notice."

"All those twins are Seers. Like you, they all have preternatural abilities or powers."

"Pre-what? What kind of power?"

"Power that is unnatural. Usually having to do with psychic abilities or extraordinary strength and speed." Raphael finishes and stares at me intently.

"What do you mean? Do all twins have special powers? How come I've never felt supernatural? Can I fly?" The words gush out of my mouth. I shift myself around in the chair, cross my legs, and draw my knees up to my chin. I hold my breath; I'm not a hundred percent sure I want to hear his answers.

"You definitely can't fly and shouldn't try to. Nor are you supernatural," Raphael says with a smile. "In fact, you're completely human. You just have powers or abilities beyond those of a normal human. And, no, not all twins are Seers. Only the chosen few, the direct descendants of Lilith. And a Seer's powers are strongest during their teenage years. They tend to diminish afterward."

"So I have superhuman teen girl powers?" I ask.

I suddenly feel like Wonder Woman. Or Jessica Jones. Maybe I should be slinking around in a sexy, one-piece outfit *à la* Cat Woman instead of my usual Converse and jeans.

Raphael shakes his head. "Seers' abilities are generally both physical *and* psychic. They sometimes dream things, like future events, or read people's thoughts. And their strength and speed is often much greater than that of the average human."

"Cool," I say. "I'd love to be able to know what people are thinking. It would be a bit like having X-ray vision."

"Well, the ability to read minds is not always consistent. Like radio waves, the thoughts can sometimes be disjointed and unclear."

"That sucks," I say, sticking my lower lip out in a mock pout.

Raphael frowns. "You need to take this seriously. These powers are a gift, and they are important. Demons and dark forces are gaining power again. And this time things may be different. This time we may be heading toward the final battle. If that is the case, only the chosen Seers can save humankind."

"Final battle?" I ask.

"Fresh, ice-cold lemonade," my mother practically sings as she swoops into the room, balancing a tray of glasses. I stare at her. It's easy to see the dancer she once was in the way she moves across the room, gracefully setting the tray down on our battered coffee table. Ice cubes clink together in the glasses.

She hands a glass to Raphael first, then me, before settling herself on the sofa.

"Thank you. This is perfect," Raphael says.

I take a sip of the lemonade, observing Mom over the rim of my glass. Her face is flushed with colour, and the dark circles under her eyes have disappeared. She looks healthy enough to be on the cover of a fitness magazine.

"You look great, Mom," I say, putting my glass back on the table. "Your doctors must be really happy."

Mom smiles. "They're not just happy, Jazz. They're amazed. What's happening to me is nothing short of a miracle."

"What do you mean?" I ask.

"My kidneys seem to be spontaneously healing themselves. And the lupus seems to be going into remission; there is an undetectable level of antibodies in my system. The doctors have no medical explanation for it. They tested me today."

I'm like a computer crashing; my mind can't comprehend what she's telling me. Mom is getting better. And she's recovering from chronic kidney failure, which is pretty much impossible without a transplant.

"That's fantastic," Raphael says. "A second lease on life."

"It looks that way," Mom replies. "But I'm definitely not going to waste this miracle. Every moment of every day, I'm going to live life to the fullest." She pauses and smiles. "Tomorrow, I am going to start to dance again. Who knows? If everything goes well, I may realize my dream of owning a dance studio."

Tears well up in my eyes. I leap off the chair, run over, and throw my arms around her neck. I can't remember the last time I felt this happy.

"When did you start feeling better?" I ask.

Mom leans back into the sofa and looks thoughtful. "You know what?" she says. "When I really think about it, it's been so recent, so sudden." She looks over at Raphael. "This sounds crazy, but I remember starting to feeling better shortly after meeting you and Mike."

"Really?" Raphael says, raising his eyebrows in surprise. "What a coincidence."

I look over at him. Though he ignores my gaze, I know he feels me watching.

He knows a lot more than he's letting on about Mom's miraculous recovery. It's clearly not just some happy coincidence — nor is Mr. Jones's dirty old dog's vanishing tumour.

In fact, since Raphael arrived on the scene, a lot of strange things have happened. It makes me wonder just who he is. And, if I'm really honest, a good part of me wonders *what* he is because it seems like he has some pretty special powers of his own.

"Who do you and your brother live with?" I ask.

"Our other brother, Gabe, who's away at the moment. Why?"

"What about your mom? Your dad?" I ask, raising an eyebrow at him.

"Jasmine," Mom says, her voice sharp. "Mind yourself."

"That's okay," Raphael says. "But if you don't mind, Jazz, I'd rather not talk about it right now." He shoots me a wide, completely fabricated smile.

That's when I decide I will attend Beaconsfield after all. I want to find out more about Raphael and his brothers. And I need to learn more about this Seer stuff, the Place-in-Between, and most importantly, how to get Jade back.

CHAPTER 12

Apparently, the crazy secretary actually works at Beaconsfield, not Riverdale. Nothing surprises me anymore.

"Good morning, Jasmine," she says as I walk into the office. She's standing beside a photocopier behind the main desk. "Need a late slip, I take it?"

I stare at her. "Don't you work at another school?"

She stops whatever she's doing at the photocopier and walks over to the desk. "You mean Riverdale? No, I was just over there making sure you made it here. I guess you could say I had a cameo appearance." She laughs loudly.

I grimace. I've only been in this place about two minutes, and already the weirdness has started.

"Yeah, I need a late slip," I say, looking over at the clock. It's already 9:15. Sleeping was hard last night. Every muscle in my body screamed with pain any time I moved even slightly. The pain woke me up so many times I lost count. I overslept my alarm by an hour this morning.

"Glad to see you made the decision to attend here," the secretary says as she initials the late slip. "And it's a much better choice you're making today by showing up. We really don't encourage skipping classes." She smiles widely, like an airline hostess who's just offered me pretzels and a soft drink.

"You know I skipped school yesterday?" I ask. "How come no one called my mom?"

"My sister saw you downtown. We find it's better to discuss your poor decision-making here at school with you, rather than worrying your mother."

"Your sister saw me?" I ask. "How did your sister know who I was?"

"She's a bit, how shall I put this? Eccentric."

"That still doesn't explain how she knew. Seriously, how did you know where I was?"

The secretary answers me with a smile and silence.

I glare at her, annoyance building up in me like a sneeze, and suddenly it hits me. The woman outside the subway yesterday — the one with the badly bleached hair and startling blue eyes — she was familiar because she looked so much like this woman. They're clearly twins.

"Does your sister have some ..." I pause, trying to think of the most polite way to ask my question. "Mental illness?"

She laughs again, and this time the laugh ends with a little snort. "Don't let my sister fool you. She might come across as crazy, but she's saner than most people. The reason she stays on the streets and in the underground is because she sees and hears things most people miss. She's our eyes and ears here at Beaconsfield."

For the first time, the secretary's mood grows serious. "My sister reported to us that you were extremely reckless yesterday. You need to listen to your Protectors. Things are changing. The Earth is in trouble, and these climate disasters and the subsequent shifting in human populations are only part of it. There's talk that demons are with us. Talk that they are walking amongst humans again. That's why we're gathering as many Seers at Beaconsfield as we can."

The door to the office opens, and a tall, thin woman enters, followed by two girls.

"I guess I'd better get to class," I say.

"Yes, you should," the secretary replies. "You have a huge amount to learn in a very short time, Jasmine."

"So I've been told," I mutter, taking the late slip and turning to leave. I walk toward the woman and her daughters. Surprise, surprise — they're identical twins.

"Good morning," the secretary says to them in a sing-song voice. "Welcome to Beaconsfield."

"Good morning," the woman replies. Her words are heavily accented. "We're so grateful to be here. We've just arrived from South Africa and were told that this school would accept us."

And we've seen so much. So much destruction. Bloodshed. The bodies of those who died of dehydration piled along the roadside like firewood. The ravages of climate change are far worse than you in Canada can imagine.

I stare at the woman. Her lips haven't moved since she told the secretary about the school acceptance. I suddenly realize the voices I thought I'd been hearing the last few years since Jade's disappearance weren't imaginary voices at all: I've been picking up on people's thoughts.

One of the girls smiles shyly as I approach. She's much taller than me, with the straightest, whitest teeth I've ever seen; they're like pieces of Chiclets gum lined up in perfect rows.

I smile back as I walk past. They may have been through a lot, but these two have no idea what they're still in for. And, really, neither do I.

The class I'm late for is English with Mr. Khan. Great. I slink into the room like a dog with its tail between its legs. After all, the last time I saw Mr. Khan, I was running away, defiant, and totally sure I'd never return to the school.

"I was hoping you'd be back," he says with a smile.

I smile weakly and hand him my late slip. Even though I've only been gone a day, at least ten new faces turn to stare at me. The classroom is packed with students. There's barely room to move between all the desks.

I don't see Raphael anywhere, and my heart sinks with disappointment. I take a seat in the back row.

"So, to wrap up," Mr. Khan says, "I would like you to read the essay by the late Dr. Suzuki. Then you'll respond to the question, 'How might things be different today if the world had heeded his warnings?' I also need your persuasive piece on the issue of London using icebergs as a source of drinking water. Remember, you need to argue either for or against the sustainability of this practice and how fair it is to the rest of the planet."

There's a collective groan from the class. And, in a room of nearly forty, it's a loud groan. Since I have no idea what Mr. Khan is talking about, I just sit there, looking around and counting the number of identical twin girls in the class.

There are ten sets altogether. Twenty twin girls. That means half the kids in this class are twins. I suppose I count as a twin too … at least sort of.

"Okay. That's enough," Mr. Khan says, clapping his hands to silence the class. "Get used to it. You're in secondary school now. And you'll be late for gym class if you continue because I can't tell you which group you're in when you're this loud."

The class quiets down. Mina raises her hand.

"What do you mean which group we're in? Don't we all go to the same gym class?"

Mr. Khan shakes his head. "Too many new students have enrolled in the past few days, so we have to split the classes. Sasha, Cyndy, Tanisha, Emily, and Menusha, you and the boys will head to the gym. The rest of the girls will be going to Ms. Samson's class in room 214."

Great. It's just my luck to be in the same group as Mina. We trudge down the hall to room 214.

Our teacher, Ms. Samson, is older than I expected. Her hair, which is pulled back in intricate cornrows, is completely grey. She's leaning against a wooden walking stick as we file in.

"Take a seat and make it fast," she says, clapping her hands together.

"Take a pill," Mina mutters, purposely scraping her chair across the floor before sitting down.

Ms. Samson's eyes narrow and she regards Mina with such coolness that I swear the air in the room drops at least ten degrees. This lady might be old, but she's intense.

"Your aggression is going to be a liability." She bangs her stick against the floor rapidly. The chestnut skin of her hands is pulled so tightly, each tendon and fragile bone becomes painfully visible as the stick makes contact with the tiled floor. The sound reverberates around the room like gunfire. A few of the girls jump in their seats, others laugh nervously.

"What does liability mean? Do any of you know?"

One girl raises her hand timidly.

Ms. Samson uses her walking stick to point at the girl. "Yes, you. What is your name?"

"Lily," the girl replies, her voice quivering.

"Lily, what does it mean if you are a liability?" Ms. Samson asks, walking over to the girl's desk and standing practically on top of her. I make a mental note not to raise my hand in this class. Ever.

"You're a disadvantage?" Lily says.

"Are you asking me or telling me?" This question is accompanied by more banging of the walking stick. I'm noticing there's a kind of rhythm to all this banging and clapping. It's almost hypnotic.

"If you're a liability, it means you're a weak point, a disadvantage to someone or something," Lily says. This time she speaks a little louder and more confidently.

"Lily, who is your sister?" Ms. Samson asks. She turns and surveys the room.

Confusion washes over Lily's face. "Um, she's right back there," she says, pointing. It's evident they're identical twins, so I can see why Lily's a bit confused by Ms. Samson's question. "Her name is Cassandra."

"And are you the eldest twin?" Ms. Samson asks, making her way back up to the front of the class.

"No," Lily replies. "Cassandra was born before me."

"So you are the reflective and cautious one," Ms. Samson says. "This is very important. You will be the one with more up here." She taps her head. A few of the girls let out muffled giggles.

"Hey!" Cassandra protests.

"Cassandra," Ms. Samson says, turning her gaze to the back of the class. "You will be the brave one, the one who will take the lead in a battle. But you need your sister because you will also have a tendency to take too many risks, to be too rash. You must balance each other at all times, for you are responsible for a shared soul."

Okay. This woman is a complete wacko. What the hell is wrong with this place? Do they hire from local mental health institutions? And what does any of this have to do with gym class?

Ms. Samson turns, walks over the computer, and types something. She whirls back around and, using her walking stick, points at the sentence projected across the whiteboard. My heart misses a beat as I read it:

YOU ARE THE SEERS.

CHAPTER 13

"What we do in this class is not to be discussed with any other students here at Beaconsfield or elsewhere. Not under any circumstances. Is that clear?" Ms. Samson says, surveying the class. "As far as the other students in this school are concerned, this is simply a girls' physical education and health class. This includes your boyfriends or, if you are so inclined, your girlfriends. Your very lives may depend on this information being kept secret."

I'm still staring at the words on the board, and at one in particular. *SEERS*.

And what is this stuff about sharing a soul?

The entire class is murmuring. They're likely wondering how to get away from this crazy woman. I look around. Every single girl in the class has an identical twin. Except for me. And Mina.

I glance over at Mina. Her face is a perfect picture of fury. She looks like a volcano that's about to explode.

"What are you talking about? This is crazy," she snaps, standing up and gripping the sides of her desk tightly as she speaks. "I want the principal to come in here because you're delusional. This is supposed to be a *gym* class. G-Y-M."

Ms. Samson leans back against the wall, her arms folded across her chest, watching Mina. A tiny smile tugs at the corners of her lips.

"This is crazy," Mina repeats, this time speaking more to the class than to Ms. Samson. She looks around at all of us, even me. I'm shocked to see she's shaking and seems nervous. "We can't just let her say all of this wacked-out stuff to us."

Unbelievably, I feel for Mina. This is how I felt when Raphael grabbed me in London (well, in the London that is the Place-in-Between) and told me all that crazy stuff about demons, Limbo, and Jade.

Except it all doesn't seem quite as crazy anymore. Not after what I saw, and was chased by, down there. I don't like the talk about twins sharing one soul and stuff, either, but I want to know more. If there's anything that Raphael's taught me, it's that shutting out information just because I don't want to hear it is stupid ... and dangerous. Plus, if this woman is some sort of expert on Seers, she might be able to tell me more about what's happened to Jade ... and how to get back to her.

"Are you quite done?" Ms. Samson asks. She unfolds her arms and walks slowly toward Mina, the walking stick thudding heavily on the floor in time with each footfall, as if to signal her approach. Mina is still standing, her hands firmly clamped on either side of her desk. It's like watching a lion slowly stalking its prey.

Ms. Samson stops. "I am sorry about what happened to your sister and mother, Mina. I know it's left you scared and powerless."

My blood turns to ice. I look at Mina. The colour has drained from her face, leaving her skin an ashy grey. She opens and closes her mouth several times, like a goldfish that's been tossed out of its bowl. No sound comes out.

"Your sister's death has left you with half a soul. And, make no mistake, a Seer with half a soul is in an incredibly vulnerable and precarious place. But deep down, in the very pit of your half-soul, you already knew this. Didn't you, Mina?"

I watch as big, fat tears cling to the bottom lashes of Mina's eyes like reluctant suicides, then drop and roll down her cheeks. Her bottom lip is quivering. She slowly nods her head.

"Stop blaming yourself for what happened. It was solely your mother's decision. We're here to keep you safe. Or, at least as safe as we can under the present circumstances." She raps the walking stick loudly against the floor. As if on cue, Mina crumples into her seat with her fists tightly balled at her sides. She keeps her head down, her hair hiding her face, but I know she's crying. I can see the slight heaving of her shoulders.

By the time we leave Ms. Samson's class, my head is reeling. Apparently, not all twin girls are Seers. She confirmed some of what Raphael told me: Seers are genetically connected to this chick called Lilith, who was apparently Adam's wife before Eve. She's gotten a bad rap over the centuries because she held supernatural powers and led armies into battle, refusing to be subservient to men. Good for her, right? But because she used her girl power without shame and men could not control her, they made up nasty rumours about her. Rumours that she was a demon, a vampire, and an evil whore. Yeah, I know what you're thinking: not a lot has changed between guys and girls over the years. Kind of depressing. Instead of spreading this stuff on social media, guys back in the day wrote trashy rumours on scrolls and cave walls. Nice.

Protectors are people chosen to trace the lineage of Seers around the world and to, well, protect us. Usually there are no more than a couple dozen Seer twins born in a generation, if that. Many of the Protectors are actually older Seers. I guess they go into protecting, instead of retirement.

Ms. Samson even told us that the witch trials came about because of Seers. People thought these young women had cloned themselves to spread more of their evil, demonic powers. Powers like warning them about impending plagues, et cetera. Seems to me they should've been thanking the Seers, not throwing them in boiling water and burning them alive at the stake.

I'm so deep in thought about all of this I don't even notice that someone has fallen into step with me.

"Penny for your thoughts," Raphael says.

I look up, startled. He smiles at me. I smile back, mesmerized by the deep green of his eyes; they're the colour of spring grass. I've never seen eyes as green and vibrant as his. Not even on a cat.

Self-consciously, I smooth my hair with one hand.

"Just came from Ms. Samson's class," I say. "Interesting woman."

"I know all of this must be pretty overwhelming," he says. "But it will become easier to deal with the information you're getting."

"How do you know about all of *this*?" I stop walking and look him directly in the eye. "We've been practically threatened with beheading if we tell any other students what goes on in that class. What makes you so different than everyone else at this school?"

"I can't tell you that, Jazz," Raphael answers. He looks down for a moment, and I swear I see a glimmer of longing in his eyes. He wants to tell me more; I can feel his desire to, even though it's unsaid.

His head snaps up and he looks straight at me. "You're not supposed to be able to do that with me," he says. His voice is hard but also tinged with something else. Fear? Panic?

"Do what?" I ask. I'm genuinely surprised. I haven't done anything that I know of. And Raphael has never spoken to me this way before.

"Hello, you two," Ms. Samson interrupts. She's standing just to the side of us, running her fingers along the beads of one of the many necklaces adorning her neck. "Jasmine, may I speak with you?" she asks.

I look at Raphael. He nods at me. "Sorry," he says. "I guess I'm just a bit off today. Go ahead. We'll speak later."

He smiles, clearly trying to reassure me about what just happened. I don't feel better, though. Instead, I get the feeling that something just changed between us forever.

CHAPTER 14

"You saw Jade the other night?" Ms. Samson asks. We're back in her classroom. She's closed the door behind us.

I sit on top of one of the desks and let my knapsack slide off my shoulders onto the chair behind me. "Yeah," I reply. "How do you know?"

Ms. Samson comes and sits on top of the desk across from me. It's a nice gesture; it makes us seem equal. Not many teachers would do something like that.

"Raphael told me. I take it he was there with you?" she asks.

I nod. "He saved me from the creatures … the demons or whatever. But I left Jade there…. Is she a lost soul?" As soon as I ask this question, tears blur my vision, and I quickly look down at my hands. I don't really know this lady, and certainly don't want to be crying in front of her.

"Raphael didn't save you, Jasmine," she says. "He can't save you. He can guide you and guard you to a degree, but you saved yourself down there. You just need to remember how."

I look up at her. "Believe me," I say, "I didn't save myself. The last thing I remember is that I was about to be some demon's dinner. Raphael definitely saved me." I can't help smiling at the sound of his name.

Ms. Samson frowns at me. "Raphael is supposed to be your guide right now until we can find out what is happening with Jade. But …" She regards me carefully. "I am not sure it's a good idea."

"Why?" I ask. "He's helped me a lot with all of this."

She regards me carefully. "You're a Seer. You mustn't let feelings develop for Raphael. He is your guide, your guardian. That's all."

My face goes hot. How does she know? Is she a Protector? Or am I so transparent with my feelings that I might as well have I heart Raphael scrawled across my forehead?

"We're just friends," I lie. "Sometimes he even gets on my nerves."

Ms. Samson watches me for a moment, the brown fingers of her right hand delicately tracing one of her beaded necklaces.

"Fine," she says. I know she doesn't believe me. "You likely won't be alone with him again, anyhow. Tonight you, Raphael, Cassandra, and Lily will make an attempt to return to the Place-in-Between to rescue your sister."

My heart skips a beat. "Jade? But she's dead, isn't she?"

"She can't be, or you wouldn't be so powerful. Mina's powers are almost non-existent because her sister is dead. No, the other half of your soul still lives."

"Then why is she in Limbo?" I ask.

Ms. Samson sighs. "From what Raphael said, it appears she might be trapped there. Did you have contact with your sister at any time whilst you were in the Place-in-Between?"

"Of course," I say. "I saw her on the staircase, right before …" I trail off, remembering the sickening thud of bodies and pained screams as people tumbled down the station's stairs.

"I know that you saw her, but did you physically come in contact? Did you touch?"

I nod. "She grabbed my hand as she began to fall." I pause for a moment. "But I couldn't hold on. There were too many bodies." My bottom lip quivers as I think about Jade's face when we were separated from one another on the stairwell.

"I'm sorry to keep asking you about this," Ms. Samson says, her voice softening. "But her hand? Did it feel like flesh and blood? Was it warm?"

I'm confused. "Of course. But we were still pulled apart, and I lost her. That's when Raphael grabbed me and took me away."

Ms. Samson gets up and walks toward the front of the room, her walking stick clicking in unison with each footstep.

"The bodies you felt on the stairs were nothing more than energy, negative energy, emanating from the spirits that are stuck in the Place-in-Between. Whether they are afraid or angry, their denial of death keeps them trapped there. Of course, this energy can be very strong, especially when it is collective. The molecular composition of the lost souls and inorganic matter in the Place-in-Between is different than any state of matter on Earth. It's closest to plasma, but of a higher density. You can interact with them, but you will feel a difference."

Ms. Samson stops for a moment. I feel her hesitating. She's not sure if she should tell me everything. "But your sister Jade is there, in the Place-in-Between, in body, not just in spirit. And we really don't know how this happened. Regardless, the darker forces seem to be holding her hostage."

Then it hits me. Jade has spent all these years trapped in that horrible place, unable to return home. I think about the nights I've fallen asleep to the sound of Mom's quiet weeping in the bedroom next to mine. Jade's disappearance did such damage to Mom's health; the doctors always suspected her lupus was triggered and worsened by the stress of my sister's abduction. But at least Mom and I had each other. What has Jade gone through?

"I know this is a lot to take in," Ms. Samson says, interrupting my thoughts. "And we have no idea how they are keeping her with them. But you must try to go back down tonight and bring her back. Jade needs to be here in the land of the living."

"I don't know how I got there, though," I say. Every cell in my body is screaming with fear, and I don't want to go back to face those creatures. But in my heart I know I have to. Jade needs me.

"We suspect travelling on the subway did it," Ms. Samson says. "The underground systems that extend under the great cities of the world have long been used as gateways by demons when they become strong enough to cross over. Before that, it was caves, crypts, and tunnels. Perhaps it is because these things are closer to the Underworld. You see, the Place-in-Between is but a layer in the fabric; there are places much darker and more dangerous. The way you can get there and back is to visualize where you want to be. All Seers can do this. That's why we're sending Lily and Cassandra with you. For extra support in case you are attacked, and because they've done well when their concentration and powers of visualization were tested in class."

Ms. Samson's eyes grow serious. "What you are about to do tonight is extremely risky, Jasmine. We must never lose twin Seers at the same time to demons, but we need to send Lily and Cassandra with you. Together, they are stronger as a pair. All of you are stronger when you are with your twin."

"What happens if twin Seers are killed at the same time?" I ask. She hasn't mentioned that Jade and I will also be together, though that is precisely what she's thinking. I can read this thought clearly in her mind.

"Demons can inhabit human bodies, if they become strong enough," Ms. Samson says. "But they need to take over one whole soul in order to do so. If both Seers are killed at the same time, they can drain the shared soul of its powers and inhabit the bodies."

I think about this for a moment. "You mean, like, evil Seers would be walking around? Demon Seers?" In my mind I'm imagining just what this might mean. A super demonic, mean girl? It's not pretty.

Ms. Samson slowly nods. "Yes, demon Seers with the power to read human minds, to dream prophetically, and most importantly, with the ability to destroy super-natural beings that belong to the forces of good, as well as those that belong to the darkness. I wish you luck and strength tonight, Jasmine. I have no idea what might await you in the Place-in-Between, but you mustn't let fear or other negative emotions rule your thoughts. Remember, that is what makes the dark forces strong."

Then Ms. Samson gets up, walks to her desk, and sits down in front of an enormous pile of marking. And, just like that, she becomes an ordinary teacher again. As she picks up her red pen to begin scrawling comments on students' work, I grab my knapsack and silently leave, hoping I will live to see her tomorrow.

CHAPTER 15

Raphael messages all three of us with instructions to meet him at seven o'clock outside Bay Station. I was hoping to bump into him after leaving Ms. Samson's class, just to talk to him about everything, but wasn't able to find him anywhere. I couldn't help being disappointed. I know I'm not supposed to have feelings for him, but really, what harm is there in me having a little crush? I don't understand why Ms. Samson is so freaked out about it. A guy as hot as Raphael isn't going to go for someone like me anyway. Even if I am kind of a superhero.

Before I leave the apartment, I give Mom a massive hug and kiss. After all, I may never see her again. This nearly starts me blubbering, especially when I think of Mom dealing with the loss of another daughter. I know that would kill her. Literally.

On the flip side, if we are successful, I won't be coming back alone. The possibility of returning Jade to Mom makes the danger I'm about to face more than worth it.

"What is all of this hugging me like a boa constrictor about?" she asks, laughing. Her brown eyes sparkle; she's getting healthier by the day. "Did you do something wrong in school? Should I expect a call any minute?"

"I just want you to know how much I love you," I say, my throat tightening. "How lucky I feel to have such a great mom."

"I'm lucky as well," she replies, hugging me back. "Now go and meet your friends. What did you say their names are?"

"Cassandra and Lily. And Raphael's going to be there too."

Mom raises an eyebrow at me. "I think he likes you, *mija*"

I shake my head. "No, Mom, I really don't think he does," I say, remembering how he pushed me away when I tried to kiss him.

"How could he not like my beautiful daughter? Besides, I've noticed the way he looks at you." She winks at me. "Now go and meet your friends and have fun."

If only she knew.

The sun is just setting, casting long shadows in front of me as I power walk. Sweat rolls down my face and drips into my eyes, making them sting like crazy. Even the sun slipping below the horizon doesn't seem to affect the temperature much anymore; the air is still heavy and hot. Cicadas sing from the trees.

I'm over ten minutes late and everyone is already waiting for me outside the station. Cassandra makes a point of looking at her watch.

"Sorry," I say, breathlessly. I'm hoping I don't have massive pit stains on my T-shirt.

"Not a worry," Raphael says, smiling at me. "You're not that late, and I've just finished filling these two in on what we might expect."

I look at him. "What should we expect? Will it be the same as last time we were there?"

"I really don't know," Raphael says. "But if we are able to get through the gateway, we'll be back in London. At what point in history we arrive, is uncertain. What is guaranteed is that it will be a time when there was an abundance of negative energy and human suffering."

"How do we get through the gateway?" Cassandra asks. She takes a clear elastic band out of her jeans pocket and twists her long, glossy black hair back off her face and into a loose bun. I can't help noticing how angular her face is and how beautiful she looks with her hair off her face. A twinge of jealousy runs through me like a shock; I hope Raphael isn't noticing this as well. "Is it like a magic door or something that suddenly opens up?" I detect a slight sarcastic edge to her words. Clearly she doesn't believe everything she's been told. Not that I blame her. Even seeing this stuff with my own eyes wasn't enough to convince me at first.

"I didn't see anything — I mean there was no door or gate or anything like that," I reply as the four of us descend into the subway station. We hit our cards against the fare readers and head down the next set of steps. "I thought it was just another power failure happening. But when the lights came back on, I was in London during the Second World War. Or at least, that's where I thought I was."

We stop at the southbound platform. I have a feeling it doesn't really matter what direction we travel or which train we get on. The usual smattering of commuters are milling around us, waiting impatiently. It's early in the evening, so there are still loads of business people in suits wanting to get home, their faces red and sweaty from the heat.

Business people hardly ever used to use public transit, but since the government began charging fifty dollars, per trip, to drive cars in the city, that's changed. It was one of the things they did a few years ago to try to stop climate change. But it was far too little, too late.

Lily is nervously biting her fingernails. She glances over at me. "How are we supposed to get to your sister if there are demonic things down there waiting for us?" she asks.

"I'm not exactly sure," I admit. "But Raphael says they can't hurt us unless they become powerful. Negative feelings, like fear and anger, are their power source." I don't tell her how my fear made one of them strong enough to grab me in a vise-like grip as I ran along the tracks. Some things are better left unsaid.

"Well, that's not good, because if any of this stuff is real, I'm going to be pretty scared." She looks at me with wide eyes. "Actually, forget the future tense. I'm totally scared right now."

There's a low rumbling from inside the tunnel, and a shimmer of light appears. The next train is approaching. I'm relieved because I don't have anything to say to make Lily feel better.

The train slides alongside the platform. We walk on, find seats, and sit down. Cassandra is beside Raphael. It makes sense. I was talking to Lily just before we got on. Still, that little twinge of jealousy rears its ugly head again.

"What do we do now?" Cassandra asks as the subway car makes its next stop. I watch about a dozen people get off, only to be replaced by new travellers.

Raphael looks at me. "Think about Jade," he says. "Try to visualize her the way she was when you saw her on the stairwell. Maybe that will help connect the two of you."

I'm so scared. I want to go and rescue Jade, but I'm afraid of what we're going to need to face in order to get to her. I can't be this afraid when we cross over.

"Do it, Jazz," he says, this time more gently. "We're here together. If anything happens, just remember you can battle demons. All Seers can."

"Should we really be having this crazy conversation here," Cassandra asks, jerking her head in the direction of the other passengers, "in public?"

"This lot will just think we're talking about some new video game or something," Raphael says. "Not to worry."

But I am worried. Worried because I wasn't able to keep my fear under control last time I was sucked into the Place-in-Between, and I have a strong feeling that Cassandra and Lily won't be able to either. Especially Lily. So, if three Seers are down there feeling terrified, won't that make the demons super-strong?

"How do we battle them?" I ask. "With our bare hands? In case you haven't noticed, I'm all of five foot three and weigh a hundred pounds."

"The three of you have strength that you don't yet realize," Raphael says. "Demons need to be beheaded. That will kill them."

"Oh, God," Lily says, putting her hand to her mouth. She looks like she might be sick.

"We don't have much time," Raphael says. "We need to find Jade and get her out of there. It's no place for the living."

"That's what I thought!" I say, leaning over Cassandra and grabbing his arm. "Just before we ended up back here."

"Go on, Jasmine. She's still alive. If the gateway is open, we can get her."

I grit my teeth, take a deep breath, and close my eyes. I try to picture my sister on the stairs of the London subway station the moment before she grabbed my hand.

I can see Jade in my mind, making her way down the steps at Bethnal Green station, her eyes meeting mine.

Lily screams as the subway lurches to one side. The train seems to be navigating a sharp turn in the tracks. I'm tempted to open my eyes, but force myself to continue thinking of Jade.

The crazy thing is, Jade is no longer on the stairs. In my mind, she's now running down a narrow, cobbled street. She keeps looking back over her shoulder, as though she's running from someone. Or something. She's wearing a long, embroidered velvet dress with puffy sleeves and a high collar. Her dark hair trails out behind her as she runs. Her eyes are pools of terror. The vision is so real I feel like I could reach out and touch her.

"Get me off of here!" Lily screams as the subway lurches again. Her voice sounds distant, though, as if she's far away from me, yelling through a dense fog.

There's a sudden screeching of brakes and we're all thrown forward. I open my eyes.

Everything is dark, like night without a moon.

CHAPTER 16

The first thing that hits me is the stench. It's the grossest, most disgusting stink I've ever smelled in my life. It's worse than puke, rotting garbage, and dirty gym equipment all mixed together.

"Oh, my God," Lily says before turning over on her side and vomiting onto the cobbled street.

I sit up. My hands are filthy from lying in the wet and dirt. At least I hope this brown stuff on my palms is just dirt.

"Get out of the way, you ne'er-do-wells!" a deep voice says from somewhere above us. "Drunk on cheap ale, are you? Well, out of my way!"

I look up. A man is walking toward us, a scraggly looking horse beside him. The horse's head droops like a flower without enough water, and the bags it carries on either side of its skinny body seem far too heavy for it.

We scramble to our feet, self-consciously wiping our hands on the front of our clothes. We're all wearing dresses now, except for Raphael who has on knee-length pants.

The man spits on the ground as he passes us. "Get ye up and to church, young ruffians. Some of us honest men are trying to make a living at market."

"Screw you," Cassandra hisses. The man either doesn't hear her, or this comment just proves to him that we're a bunch of low-life drunks. Lily puking all over likely didn't help convince him otherwise either.

A light drizzle of rain is falling. Lily moans softly to herself. Her long, black hair hangs like a limp curtain over her face.

"Okay," I say, trying to breathe through my mouth as I speak so I don't have to take in the smell of this place. "Where are we? I mean, is this London?" I scratch at my arms as I speak. The dress I'm wearing is so itchy. There are layers and layers to it, so it's hard to find any relief.

"This is definitely London," Raphael says, looking around the narrow street at the wooden houses looming over us. "I'd say we're somewhere in the mid-seventeenth century by the looks of things."

"But London doesn't have wooden houses," Cassandra says haughtily. She cocks her head to one side. "We've been there with our family. Everything is old and made of stone or brick, or new and made of glass. These," she says, waving a hand at the houses that crowd on either side of us, "are not the type of houses found in London."

"Actually, this is precisely the type of housing they had prior to the Great Fire," Raphael replies. "Which puts us somewhere before 1666."

Cassandra snorts. "That's insane."

I can barely follow their conversation. I'm itchy everywhere now. This is even worse than when I had the chicken pox. I wiggle my body around in the dress, hoping the itching will stop.

"I think I'm allergic to this dress," I say. "Is it made of wool?" At that moment, I notice Lily scratching at her arms and stomach as well. As she scratches, she's letting out this weird, low moaning sound. I have to say I'm worried about her having my back in a battle with demons. She seems like the type of girl who might lose it at the sight of a tiny spider.

"You're not going to like this," Raphael begins, "but there's so much overcrowding and such poor hygiene during this time…."

I arch an eyebrow at him. "You saying I don't shower?"

He ignores me. "People tend to keep their animals inside as well. Especially the poor." Raphael stops for a moment, as though deciding whether to tell me anything else. "It's probably fleas, Jazz. Could be bed bugs and lice, too. Most people during this time period are covered with them."

"Oh, God," Lily moans. "I can't do this. Fleas? I need to get back … now." Her voice is becoming increasingly high-pitched. "This can't be happening."

I shoot Lily a warning look. "Control yourself," I say, trying to keep my voice low.

"We need to go," Cassandra interjects. "That man is going to tell everyone in the market about us. We're strangers; we're dangerous. He thinks we've got the plague and that's why we were lying in the road, sick."

I stare at her. "How do you know all of that?"

She shrugs her shoulders. "I could read his thoughts. They just sort of jumped into my mind as he walked away."

"Cassandra's right. We should get going," Raphael says. "It's not safe for us to stay in one place for long."

We begin to walk. Raphael's words have made us quieter. Noise crowds in all around us, making it hard to have a conversation anyway. People are shouting, hanging laundry out of windows, and throwing rancid liquid and garbage into the filthy gutters along the street. Disgusting smells fill the air all around us.

I look over at Cassandra as we walk. She's strutting along, all attitude and confidence, but her eyes are narrowed and wary. It bugs me that she was able to hear that man's thoughts and I wasn't. She made it sound so easy. Like a podcast being switched on in her head. If I'm a Seer, why didn't I hear what he was thinking as well?

"Oi, you!" A woman that is all soft mounds of flesh and red-faced with boils bounds toward us from the other side of the street. My heart does a nervous flip-flop. Her sunken eyes are fixed firmly on me.

I glance over at Raphael. He's carefully watching the woman's approach. Considering how huge she is, she's surprisingly fast. A scrawny chicken crosses in front of her, and she pauses for only a moment in order to kick it out of the way with the finesse of a professional soccer player. The bird skitters across the cobblestones in a blur of feathers and indignant squawks.

"You!" she shouts, wagging a doughy finger at me. People turn to stare. I look hard at her, trying to determine whether or not she is one of the demonic creatures. Doesn't look like she is.

She rushes up to me, grabs me by the front of my dress, and begins to shake me. My head snaps back uncomfortably. I didn't think lost spirits could have this much strength. I guess I was wrong.

"Hey!" Cassandra shouts. "Get your hands off of her, freak."

"Who are these people?" the woman asks me. Cold spittle flies onto my face, making me want to barf. "We sent ye to Woolwich. Why are ye still here?"

My head bobs back and forth on my neck like a yo-yo. I can't even catch my breath. I try to speak, to tell this tank of a woman that I have no idea what she's talking about, but can't even open my mouth.

Suddenly Cassandra is beside me. "I said, get your hands off her, you fat freak!" she shouts, thrusting her hands at the woman's massive chest.

Her boobs are huge, like giant sacks of rice.

I watch as Cassandra struggles to get a firm grip on the woman. The woman's eyes widen, and she loosens her grip on me. Cassandra pulls her hands back with a startled yelp.

"She's a spirit. Different molecular energy from us," I say to Cassandra.

"Get thee to Woolwich," the woman says, turning her attention fully to me. The look of shock on her face mirrors that on Cassandra's. "The plague is upon your house."

"I think she's quoting Shakespeare," Lily says, her voice low. "She's cursing us, isn't she?"

"No," says Cassandra. "Over a thousand people have died in London this past week from the plague. It's killed many of her neighbours, and her local parish has nearly been wiped out. They've closed the churches, and the court and even the royal family has fled. She thinks that Jasmine should already be in Woolwich for some reason."

The woman stares at Cassandra, her mouth gaping open. "How do ye know this? How is it that you can steal mine thoughts?" she demands, her face reddening. Understanding sweeps across her face. "Witches! You lot are witches! That's how YOU" — she points her finger at me again, and this time there's fear, not anger, in her eyes — "are in two places at once."

People have stopped what they're doing; a crowd is beginning to form. The word "witches" has definitely made people more interested in what's happening. And in us. Concerned murmuring fills the air.

"We're not witches," Lily says, her voice trembling.

The woman swings around and faces Lily. "Ye witches have caused all of this Black Death around us."

The murmuring is getting louder. Out of the corner of my eye, I see that many of the people are moving closer, forming a circle around us. There's a look in their eyes that I don't like. It's a mixture of fear, anger and … the need for revenge. They're like a swarm of killer bees.

"Off with their 'eads!" one man yells. Two or three people join in, and soon there is a chorus chanting for us to be decapitated.

Cassandra moves closer to me. "They want to kill us," she says. "Can they do that? I mean, they're dead, right?"

"I don't think they can," I say. But then I notice what, at first glance, looks like a harmless elderly couple joining the crowd. I nod toward them. "But those two definitely can if they're strong enough."

Cassandra follows my gaze. The couple smiles at us. Their toothy grins are more barracuda than human. And their eyes are very flat and black.

CHAPTER 17

"We've got to get out of here," I whisper in Raphael's ear. "There are demons in the crowd."

He nods, not taking his eyes off of the crowd or the woman. "I know," he says out of the corner of his mouth. "The fear and anger here is so intense. It's making them strong."

"Did all these people die during the plague?" I ask. The elderly couple are slowly making their way to the front of the crowd. More people have gathered behind the original circle. We're going to have to make an escape through layers of angry spirits.

"No," Raphael replies. "But once they're in the Place-in-Between, they forget their previous lives. They hold on to the negative emotions that brought them here, but they can't remember the specific reasons for those feelings. At the moment, all these souls truly believe they are living in London during the Great Plague."

There's a loud rumble coming from the crowd now. Hundreds of voices join in a unified chant: "*WITCHES! WITCHES!*"

The large woman who started all of this lunges forward and grabs Cassandra by the arm. "I've got one!"

"THROW HER IN THE RIVER," the crowd roars.

Raphael grabs my hand. The crowd is closing in. I smell their breath. It's the smell of a thousand animals rotting. Apparently, the brushing of teeth wasn't a big thing during this time period.

Cassandra's eyes are wild with fear. Not only is her fear giving the demons strength, but it also seems to be allowing the lost souls to interact with us more fully. The woman is now dragging Cassandra away into the crowd. I look around. Lily's gone. Has she been grabbed without us even noticing?

"We need to help Cassandra." The words barely leave my lips before I feel something wrap itself around my wrist like an icy snake.

I yelp in surprise and turn. The old woman creature draws back her cracked lips.

"Mine," it says. The voice is deep and raspy.

It begins to pull me away from Raphael and into the crowd. Terror fills my body. This is how Jade must've felt. Tears spring to my eyes. Its grasp becomes stronger, and I feel my other hand slipping from Raphael's.

I need to stop being afraid. I'm feeding this creature with my fear.

My hand is torn from Raphael's, and then I'm surrounded by the mob of lost souls. They close in around me like a pack of wild dogs. Their negative energy washes over me, as elbows stab into my ribs and leather boots connect with my shins. The pain is real. I feel like crying, but blink back the tears as I stumble. It takes all my strength just to keep standing. I don't want to risk being crushed. A shiver runs through me as I remember the bodies tumbling down on top of each other on the subway steps, taking Jade along with them.

There's sudden movement and a flash of metal from behind the creature dragging me. Its head snaps violently to one side. A guttural roar fills the air, and a spray of cold liquid hits my face as the skin between the demon's neck and body tears apart. Instinctively, I close my eyes, while frantically wiping at my face with the sleeve of the dress. The liquid stings my skin and, like everything in this place, smells of death and decay.

I open my eyes again. The demon is clawing at the air above its stump of a neck. I stare, blinking back the liquid trickling down my face.

"Don't just stand there, Jasmine!" Lily is beside me. She's holding a metal pole out in front of her with both hands. It's slick with a clear, slimy liquid. Demon blood. "They're really pissed now and this pole is getting harder to keep a firm hold on."

I snap out of it. The demon sinks to the ground, gurgling sounds coming from the stump where its head used to be.

I look at Lily and then back at the crowd. She's right: they're angry. Killing what could pass for a little old lady hasn't won us any popularity contests here in jolly old Limbo-England.

Raphael is beside us. "They've taken Cassandra to the river."

Lily's eyes widen when she hears this. She places the metal pole in front of all three of us, using it like a shield to ward off the advancing crowd. "STAY BACK OR ELSE," she shouts. Her voice is strong and steady. I'm amazed.

We move sideways, toward a small alleyway between some of the houses.

"What are they going to do to her?" I ask Raphael.

"Likely something called trial by ordeal," he says. "If she sinks, they'll find her innocent of witchcraft. If she floats, they'll see that as proof she's a witch and drown her."

"A real win-win situation," I say with a grimace.

Panic claws at my throat. Things seem so much more dangerous down here this time. If the energy of the lost souls is strong enough to drag Cassandra away from us, what must the demons' powers be like?

Then, out of the corner of my eye, I see something coming for Lily. I open my mouth to shout, but my words are cut short by her screams of pain. The elderly man demon has sunk his teeth deep into her right shoulder. She drops the metal pole, which clangs noisily onto the cobblestones. There's a flurry of movement from the crowd as they rush toward it.

"Get the pole, Jasmine!" Lily screams. Tears stream down her face. Her skin is as pale as the white sleeves of her dress. Blood seeps from the demon's mouth, which is still firmly fastened onto her shoulder. Crimson stains bloom down the length of her upper arm.

I dive for the pole. My knees hit the cobblestones, sending sharp fingers of pain skittering up and down my legs. Several hands grab for it at the same time as I do. But something tells me I'm stronger. In my hands, this pole is a dangerous weapon. Even Lily was able to use it to kill the demon.

As I wrench the pole up and away from the crowd, I begin to understand. We're Seers. *I'm* a *Seer.* I can feel the power building deep inside me.

"Back!" I shout, swinging the pole at the crowd. I'm no longer afraid.

They move backward, almost in unison. There are fewer of them now. I wonder if that's because some of the lost souls went to see what's happening to Cassandra. As soon as I think it, a vision of her pops into my head. She's being dragged, kicking and screaming, down some stone steps. There's a river, but the water isn't very deep where they've taken her.

"At high tide we'll find out if ye is a witch," one of the men says. He's nearly as wide as he is tall, and his sausage-like fingers busily wrap thick rope around Cassandra's wrists. He spits a large gob of green phlegm out of the corner of his mouth as he finishes speaking.

We have time. Not much, but at least we're not too late. I can see in my vision that the tide is coming in, but it isn't high tide yet. I snap out of the vision, and turn my attention back to Lily. She's weakening; the demon's slowly draining the life out of her.

Grasping the pole like a martial artist, I run at the creature. He sees me and releases his teeth from Lily's flesh. She slumps to the ground, and Raphael rushes over to cradle her in his arms.

I spin the pole in my hands, smashing it into the side of the demon's head. Even though the pole doesn't feel completely solid in my hands, the upper portion of its skull collapses like a month-old jack-o'-lantern. The demon lets out an angry howl and grabs the pole.

For a moment, I'm afraid it's too strong and that I'm going to lose the pole. Then I realize that the demon can only be stronger than me if I allow it. Seers hold more power than demons. And there are two of us here, even if Lily is injured.

"No!" I shout, grabbing the pole back. The demon's eyes widen. Do I see fear?

It doesn't matter. I bring the pole down and across the demon's neck, using it like a baseball bat.

THWACK!

The pole slices through the demon's neck. The creature lets out a bubbling, gurgling howl as its head falls to the cobblestones.

"They've killed both Mister and Missus MacTaverty!" shouts a man from the crowd. "An eye for an eye! Off with their heads!" There's a communal roar of anger.

I look over at Raphael and Lily. He's holding her injured shoulder, trying to stop the bleeding. Her lips are a bluish colour, and her eyes are barely open. All I can see are the whites. We can't possibly run. I don't even know if she's alive. And we're still in danger.

I turn back to the smattering of people still left. Several are moving forward.

"Stop!" I say, holding my pole beside me like a spear. "If you do not leave us immediately, I will put the curse of the plague upon every single one of your houses."

Everyone slows. They look around, giving nods of encouragement to one other. But I can see the fear and doubt creeping into their eyes. No one wants to be the first to attack.

"I mean it!" I say, putting up one of my hands, palm forward. "Leave now and I will spare your family. Continue to move toward us and expect all your loved ones dead by tomorrow."

There's concerned murmuring, and a few of the lost souls at the outer edge of the crowd slink away.

"The witches can't curse us if they're dead!" a woman bellows. I watch, holding my breath to see what the crowd's reaction will be. A few of them nod their heads in agreement, and then there's a sudden, angry rush toward us.

CHAPTER 18

"*'Twas brillig, and the slithy toves, did gyre and gimble in the wabe!*" I stop and observe the crowd. They're frozen with fear.

"She's putting the pox upon us," one man says, his voice shaking. He looks like he's about to burst into tears. "We should've left with the others whilst we could."

I raise an eyebrow at him and point for effect. "*ALL MIMSY WERE THE BOROGROVES AND THE MOME —*" Everyone begins to run, scattering in every possible direction. I watch, trying to keep a straight face.

"… *Raths outgrabe,*" I finish. My voice is hoarse from shouting. Not one of them remains. Only a small child watches us from the doorway of one of the houses. His face is a mask of dirt, and his nostrils and eyes are crusted with snot. Large, red sores cover his arms and face.

I try to smile at him, but find it impossible. How can a little kid be here, in the Place-in-Between? It doesn't seem right. No kid's spirit could be so angry or so jeal-ous or whatever else it takes to get stuck in this place.

I turn to ask Raphael why a child would be here and am shocked to see him and Lily sitting, talking, and smiling.

"'The Jabberwocky.' Nice," Lily says, pulling herself to her feet. "I love Lewis Carroll. Pretty good choice, too. I definitely feel like Alice today with all of this craziness happening. We need to get to Cassandra."

I nod, but don't respond right away to what she's just said. Instead, I stare at her shoulder. Aside from a tear in her dress, there's no other visible clue to show that she was attacked by the demon.

The three of us begin walking, careful to keep an eye out for any stray lost souls from the crowd.

"What happened to your injury?" I ask. Her eyes are sparkling, and the colour is back in her face. If anything, she looks even better than she did when we met at the subway in Toronto.

Lily frowns. "I guess I must've fallen when that demon attacked me," she says. "I tore the dress, and my shoulder feels a little bruised, but that's about it. Sorry I scared you guys. I faint sometimes when I get really nervous."

I arch an eyebrow at Raphael. "Really? She faints?" I ask sarcastically.

He looks down at the ground and pretends to be fas-cinated by a pebble or something.

Three times. The dog. Then Mom. Now Lily.

I believe in coincidences, but come on. Raphael clearly has the power to heal people and animals. The dog had cancer. Mom's last kidney was packing it in. Lupus isn't curable. Lily was badly injured. Whether she remembers or not, I know Lily was more dead than alive just a few minutes ago.

"We should be faster," Raphael says. "Cassandra needs us."

"Naw," I say. "We have all the time in the world. If she's dead, you can just bring her back to life." I walk closer to him, place my index finger under his chin, and lift his head. "Can't you?"

His emerald eyes meet mine, and for a moment, they seem to be illuminated. It's as though they are miniature suns. I shake my head. Impossible.

"Please don't do this, Jazz," he says. "Not now." He sounds so much older and more exhausted than he looks. "We've got too much to do. We need to find Cassandra."

"We've got time," I say. "The tide isn't in yet."

Our eyes remain locked for a moment, and sparks of electricity shoot through me, warming every cell in my body. I fight the desire to lean over and kiss him. Wouldn't be a wise move, in case he decides to reject me again, especially with Lily watching us. I'd die of embarrassment.

"Don't," he whispers. There's that fear again in his eyes.

"Don't what?" I ask, trying to mimic Cassandra's confidence by tossing my hair nonchalantly behind my shoulder. Some of it hits me in the mouth and sticks to my lips. Great. So much for looking confident and cool.

"I had a vision. They've tied Cassandra up by the river, and they're waiting for high tide," I say, picking the pieces of hair off my lips. "So she's not in immediate danger, but we do need to get to her."

"She could be almost anywhere along the Thames," Raphael says. "Try to connect with her again. See if there are any clues we can use to locate her."

I close my eyes and think about Cassandra. In the vision I had, she was being dragged down some stone steps at the river's edge. It hurts to think of how terrified she looked; Jade had the same look in her eyes when I had the vision of her in this place.

"Can you help me?" A tiny voice asks, interrupting my thoughts. I open my eyes. It's the little boy I saw earlier. I figure Lily and Raphael can deal with him. Poor kid. Imagine dying and then being stuck here, all alone. I close my eyes again.

Cassandra comes into view. She's sitting on the steps still, and the tide is higher now. The bottom steps have disappeared under swirling, foamy water. Rows of people are standing above her along a stone walkway. Some of them lean over, spitting and throwing sticks and bits of rotted food at her. Her arms are bound and the water is around her ankles. Her usual confidence is gone, and she is weeping quietly.

Maybe I was wrong about how much time we had to get to her.

"I *asked* if you could help me." The child's voice is gone. In its place is a deep, raspy, and completely inhuman voice.

"Oh my God," Lily whispers.

I force myself not to open my eyes. Is the child a demon? What if it attacks me? Raphael and Lily can handle this, right? I hope so, because I need to locate Cassandra….

There are buildings above where she's being held, but I can't see them clearly.

The demon's growl is intensifying.

"Hurry, Jazz," Raphael says. His voice is urgent, but controlled.

There's a bridge. Just down the river, there's this massive bridge lined with buildings and bustling with activity. Tall, wooden structures crowd unsteadily along the entire stretch of it. It's as if an entire city is jammed on there. I've never seen anything like it.

Lily screams and my eyes fly open. The demon is growling and snapping at her ankles like a rabid animal. She holds the pole in front of her, her eyes wide with fear and disgust.

"Kill it!" I shout at her. The demon is crouching lower now, as if it's getting ready to run at Lily's legs. If it grabs the pole, we're going to be defenceless. I look around for something I can use as a weapon. Other than a chicken pecking aimlessly at some bit of dirt on the cobblestones, there's not much.

"But it's just a little kid," Lily says, her voice wavering. "I can't kill a little kid."

Like a cat stalking its prey, the demon slowly crawls toward us. It growls softly, a grin playing across its crusty face. This is no kid. Black eyes gleam like glass marbles inside its face. I grab the pole from Lily.

"Then I will. It's a demon, not a child." I run at the creature and swing the pole at its neck, putting my entire weight into the movement. It hisses and skitters sideways like a crab. My pole whistles through the air, and I'm nearly thrown off-balance.

This demon is fast. Worst of all, because it's small and crouching low, it can easily protect its neck.

"Jazz, I think we better make a run for it," Raphael says, pointing at a row of houses across the road from us.

I try to keep one eye on the demon in front of me, while checking out what Raphael's talking about. My heart skips a beat. At least half a dozen more children, many of them coughing and covered with sores, are spilling out of the doorways of the houses and into the street.

"Where are we going to run to?" I ask out of the corner of my mouth. We certainly can't take on all these miniature demons.

"We need to get to the water," Raphael replies. "Since you have the pole, you'll be last. Move quickly, and don't look back unless you absolutely need to."

I swallow hard. *Don't be afraid. Don't be afraid.* I repeat the mantra in my mind, knowing that if I allow the terror that is bubbling under the surface to be felt, these demon children are going to instantly be strengthened.

"Do you know how to get to the river?" Lily asks. She's keeping her eyes on the children. They've stopped moving and are standing as still as statues, heads cocked to the right, as though intently listening to something. I wonder if they can hear us.

"Yes," Raphael replies. "You follow me, and Jasmine will bring up the rear. No one is to stop or look back. No matter what we hear or think might be happening. Understand?"

I understand. He means if something happens to me, he and Lily are not to stop.

"On the count of three," he says. "One … two —"

He doesn't even get to three before there's a loud scurrying sound as the demon children rush forward at us like an army of cockroaches.

CHAPTER 19

"RUN!"

We turn and dash down the alleyway. It's difficult to run in this dress — my feet keep getting caught in the hem, threatening to pull me down. I notice that Lily is holding her dress up in front of her as she runs. I would have to ditch the pole to do that, which would leave us without a weapon and the demons with an extra means to attack.

Raphael takes a sharp turn to the right. We're back on a busy, narrow street that's crowded with people. In the middle of the craziness, a juggler is commanding a small audience of people. One of the things he's juggling is a knife. Lily veers off and snatches the knife out of the air in one fluid motion as she passes, ignoring the cries of protest from both the juggler and the crowd.

I smile to myself. I underestimated her. She's not what she seemed.

Something grabs the back of my skirt. I stumble and catch myself from falling. I turn. It's the first demon

child, and he's latched onto my dress. He bares his pointed teeth at me and hisses like a snake.

Instinctively, I reach down with my free hand to grab
the skirt back, and that's when he sinks his teeth deep
into the fleshy part of my hand, just below my thumb. I
scream and bring the pole down like a javelin through
the top of his head.

The demon recoils in surprise, and lets go of my skirt.
I yank the pole out of its skull and turn to run again. Lily
and Raphael are now far ahead and disappearing down
a set of steps toward the water's edge.

They're leaving me. Raphael wasn't kidding. How can
he do that? I'd never leave him.

My lungs burn like hot embers in my chest, but
I can't stop running. If the demons catch me, they'll
have two captive Seers. Counting Jade, it's actually
three. And if they kill Jade and me, they'll have the entire soul of a Seer and all the power that goes with it. I
can't allow that to happen.

Somehow, deep inside myself, I know that something
is happening that is much, much bigger than just getting
Jade back. I also know that Jade and me being caught
together in the Underworld would be far more catas-
trophic than I could ever imagine.

I turn and see that the demon child is still chasing me.
The others are not far behind him, but he is too close. Too
close for me to get away with this stupid dress on.

He seems surprised when I stop. Without hesitating,
I slice the pole cleanly through his neck, screaming from
the effort.

It works. The demon's head rolls across the cobble-stones, coming to rest at the feet of a stray dog that begins to lick it enthusiastically. I turn and run to the top of the steps where I last saw Raphael and Lily.

They're climbing into a flat-bottomed, wooden boat. The guy in charge of the boat is using a long stick to push it away from the dock.

"Wait!" I shout, taking the stairs two at a time. I can hear the other demon children closing in on me. My foot catches in the hem of my dress, and this time I am unable to stop from falling. I tumble down the stairs, desperately trying to protect my head from hitting the stone steps as I fall.

I land with a thud on the dock, the pole clattering down beside me a few seconds later. My head hurts, and blood is trickling from the wounds in my hand where the demon bit me.

"Jasmine! Hurry!" Lily shouts. The boat is pulling away. I scramble up, grab the pole, gather the skirt of the dress in my injured hand, and run to the edge of the dock.

The demon children are rushing down the steps now, the first of them landing on the dock.

"Jump, Jasmine!" Raphael is standing at the front of the boat, extending his arm out toward me. Closing my eyes, I leap off the dock and into his arms, both of us falling backward into the boat. The wood creaks heavily, and for a moment, I'm afraid the bottom is going to give out from beneath us. Raphael gently takes my injured hand in his. Warm sparks of energy shoot through it like electric stars. I glance up at him in surprise.

"They should flog those little street urchins like they did back in the days of her Royal Highness, Elizabeth. God rest her soul," says the boatman. "Get out of 'ere ye little scoundrels!" he shouts as he pushes us away from the dock and out into the river.

"Yeah, they should do something like that," I say in agreement. Does he not see what they really are?

I look down at my injured hand, which Raphael is still holding. There's not even a scratch on it. It's as if the bite never happened. As casually as possible, I remove my hand from his. This stuff he's doing is beginning to really creep me out. I know I have powers, but obviously he's not your average human, either. My cards are out on the table. What's he hiding?

"Are we safe with this guy?" I whisper.

He nods. "He's just a waterman. His job is to ferry people around the Thames. Think of him as a kind of seventeenth-century taxi driver."

"Where are ye looking to lay your heads?" the water-man asks.

All three of us look at each other. We still aren't sure exactly where Cassandra is.

"I saw a bridge," I say. "It was huge, with buildings on it. Pretty tall buildings for being on a bridge." I pause, biting at my bottom lip and trying to remember more. "Does that help?"

Raphael smiles. "Good sir?" he says. "Where is the nearest bridge?"

The waterman turns. He's a tall man, with a face that is all sharp angles. His cheekbones are high and his nose and chin are large. His eyes sparkle under the shelter of two very furry, caterpillar-like eyebrows.

"There's only one bridge anywhere near here," the waterman answers. "That'd be London Bridge."

"Can you take us closer?" Raphael asks. "We need to pick up a friend there, and then we're heading to Woolwich."

I raise an eyebrow at him. Woolwich? That was the place the woman who grabbed me said I was supposed to be.

"Someone who looks identical to you has been sent to Woolwich," Raphael says, leaning in close to me. "Think about it. Who could that be, Jazz?"

Jade. I hadn't even considered the possibility that the woman mistook me for her. I thought she was just a confused lost soul intent on shaking me to death.

"We'll have to have you go on foot to get to the other side of the bridge for Woolwich, then," the waterman says. He dips his long oar into the murky water and pushes us forward, his biceps bulging. "For London Bridge is for wise men to pass over, and for fools to pass under."

We continue on in silence for a few moments. A large building that looks like a church comes into view. A noisy crowd, just like the one I saw in my vision of Cassandra, is gathered on the riverbank near it.

"What's that?" I ask the waterman, pointing toward the crowd.

"That's Southwark Cathedral, that is," he replies. "Over that way is a wild part of the city. All the thieves, actors, and unsavoury bits of the population congregate over there, they do."

"Take us over, please," I say. I can't see Cassandra, but we're still fairly far away. The water is high though. The tide has come in. That much I can tell.

The waterman raises his eyebrows at me, but he does what I've asked.

The shouting and noise get louder as we approach. And that's when I see what looks like a clump of fabric floating out and away from the water's edge, the tide drawing it farther into the river.

Lily draws in her breath. "What's that?" she whispers, grabbing my arm.

Raphael is already scrambling to the front of the boat. "Quickly!" he says, urging the waterman on. He glances over at Lily. "I think it's Cassandra."

We're pulling up alongside her now. Cassandra's black hair streams out around around her head like a halo. Lily moves beside Raphael. Together they haul her into the boat. There are cries of protest from the people on the riverbank.

"Shut up, you murderers!" Lily screams.

Raphael is gently laying Cassandra on her side. Her face is as white as printer paper. She looks completely drained of blood.

"You can't put her in 'ere," the waterman says. "She's been done for as a witch. She floats."

With the agility of a cat, Lily jumps behind him, pulls out the knife, and holds the blade against his neck. "She'll be coming in here, or *you'll* be leaving us. Understand?"

"Yes," he says, careful not to nod, so that the skin on his throat isn't sliced open.

I kneel down beside Raphael. "Turn her on her back," I say. I've done First Aid and CPR courses at school. I place a finger to Cassandra's neck. She's freezing, but there's a pulse. It's weak, but it's there.

I begin to do mouth-to-mouth. Cassandra's lips are cold. Lily watches me, eyes narrowed, from over the waterman's shoulder. She still hasn't moved the blade from his neck.

After a couple of minutes, I stop and look up. The expression on my face gives away what I'm thinking. Why isn't Raphael stepping in and using his power to heal?

"No, Jasmine. Keep going. Please," Lily begs, "don't give up yet."

I begin again. The only reason Lily and Cassandra are even in this mess is because of me. Well, me and Jade. Who made the decision to send us on this suicide mission anyway? Ms. Samson? Mr. Khan? And who says we have to risk our lives to be some sort of girl army for humanity? I don't remember signing up to be a stupid Seer.

Coughing. At first it's shallow and barely audible. Then Cassandra gives an enormous gasp, bolts upright, and begins to gulp at the air, trying to get oxygen back into her lungs. She leans over the edge of the boat and vomits.

"Holy Lazarus," the waterman says. "She is a witch come back from the dead."

"Call my sister a witch again," Lily hisses, "and it'll be the last word out of your mouth. Now take us toward Woolwich."

I don't bother reminding her that he's already dead.

CHAPTER 20

When we get to the bridge, our waterman is more than happy to get rid of us. Lily takes the blade of her knife away from his neck at the last possible moment as we disembark, but not before she makes him strip down to his undergarments, so that Cassandra can have dry clothes.

"Good riddance, ye devils," the man calls as soon as Lily is out of arm's reach.

She turns and points a finger at him. "A plague upon your house," she growls.

He blesses himself and pushes quickly away from the shore and back out into the swirling waters of the river.

We're certainly not making any friends while we're down here.

We cross over London Bridge on foot. It's like nothing I've ever seen before. There's practically an entire city on the bridge. Loads of people are crammed along it, and either side is framed with shops and businesses.

After we hire another boat, the rest of our trip is pretty uneventful. We reach Woolwich toward the end of the afternoon. The air feels damper here, and it's definitely chillier. Even though I've got on this massive dress, I still feel the cold. I guess Toronto's been sweltering for so long, my body isn't used to any temperatures below thirty degrees.

It's less crowded in Woolwich, and the smell isn't as terrible here. Though we don't say much, I get the feeling that everyone is thinking the same thing: it's going to be dark soon. We need to find Jade quickly and get out of here — if we can figure out how.

"What does the cross mean?" Cassandra asks as we pass a house with a red cross painted on the door. Her voice is still raspy, but the colour is back in her cheeks. I'm pretty proud of my CPR skills.

"Plague," Raphael replies. "Everyone in that house is quarantined for forty days and nights now. No one is allowed in and no one is allowed out. That man standing on the corner is on watch. If the people inside lower a basket from the window, he'll fill it with water and food. More importantly, he'll make sure no one escapes."

"And after forty days they let them out?" Lily asks.

Raphael's eyes darken. "During the plague, there usually wasn't anyone left to let out after the forty days were up."

"But they're already dead," I say. "They can't die of the plague, so the experience can't be that bad, right?"

Raphael shakes his head. "The thing is, they don't know they're dead, Jazz. They believe they're sick and that their loved ones are sick and dying as well. Memory is non-existent here. The lost souls flip from one difficult time in history to another." He pauses. "Do you know the story of Prometheus?"

"The guy whose liver was eaten again and again as a punishment for giving fire to humans?"

Raphael nods. "That's the one. He was chained to a mountaintop, and every day giant birds would claw his body apart. Then he'd heal, only to have it happen again the next day. It's much the same for these souls, though they have no memory of yesterday."

We walk in silence for a few moments, and I can't help remembering the raw, red sores on the demon children's faces. Being made to relive the plague over and over seems more like Hell than Limbo.

"How can children be stuck down here?" I ask Raphael. "And be demonic? It doesn't seem right. Plus, the lost souls are so much stronger this time. Look what they did to Cassandra."

Raphael pauses for a moment, and when he answers, his voice is low. I don't think he wants Cassandra and Lily to hear. It's unlikely they will, anyway; they're deep in their own conversation, walking arm in arm ahead of us.

"I don't have a lot of answers, Jazz. The lost souls seem to be doing the demons' bidding. Remember that these people's weaknesses on Earth are the reason they ended up here in the first place. They're vulnerable to dark influences. But, still, you're right. Unnatural things are happening. Any child down here likely didn't realize they'd passed. That's how they'd become a lost soul. But demon children …" He stops and shakes his head. "There are forces at work allowing the demons to take the shape of children by possessing them on Earth first."

I nod. "That's what the secretary at Beaconsfield was saying. That darker forces are at work right now. She mentioned that demons might be among us. What does that mean?"

Raphael presses his lips together tightly. "I think you and Jade might have something to do with it, but I am not certain. It could involve something even bigger. What I do know is that we need to get your sister out of here."

And that's when we hear it. Barely a whisper, but I recognize the voice right away.

"Jasmine!"

Raphael and I stop. My breath catches in my throat. It's Jade. I know it is. But where is she?

"Guys, wait a minute," I say to Lily and Cassandra. They stop and turn.

"Up here!"

This time the man guarding the quarantined house has also heard. He turns and looks sharply at us. And that's when I see something move in one of the upper windows of the house. It's a brief flash out of the corner of my eye, like a curtain fluttering in a breeze.

"You all right?" the guard asks. His voice is ripe with suspicion. I'm not surprised. We're strangers. And since there's a massive plague epidemic happening, I would be pretty suspicious of anyone I didn't know, as well.

"What family is in this house?" Raphael asks.

The guard stares hard at him for a moment, deciding whether to answer or not.

"Middleton family. Been under quarantine for twenty-five days. Basket hasn't been lowered for a week now, though. All dead, I reckon."

Raphael shakes his head. "Sorry to hear that. They had a beautiful daughter, didn't they?"

The guard shifts uneasily from one foot to the other. He looks around. "Apparently, they did. Though she didn't go in with them at the beginning. I swear she must've been brought round later." He shakes his head. "It makes no sense."

"Perhaps you didn't notice her going in with the rest of the family," Raphael says. He catches my eye before Cassandra walks closer to the guard to distract him.

That's my cue.

"I will admit, I'd had a bit too much ale down at the Queen's Head the evening before," I hear the guard say sheepishly as Lily and I sneak away behind the house.

There's a low, stone fence surrounding the back garden. The house itself is dark, and the shadows around it are lengthening. A fine mist is beginning to snake its way above the grass. It won't be long until it's completely dark.

"I'll go over first, since I'm taller," Lily says, keeping her voice low. She's already lifting her skirts and feeling for a foothold between the stones with her boot. "I can help you from the other side."

I nod. This is one of those times when being short is a total pain. I watch as Lily gracefully throws a leg over the top of the fence, then jumps down into the garden.

I pull myself up, but the skirts of my dress are heavy, and I don't have as much luck as Lily. This means I end up teetering unsteadily at the top of the fence, like an uncoordinated cowgirl learning how to ride a horse.

"Just give me your hand," Lily whispers. She reaches up to me.

I grab her hand, close my eyes, and leap. The dress twists and tangles itself around my legs as I fall, causing me to tumble toward the ground in a heap. I put my hands out to break my fall and to try to save my face.

My palms slam into the cold earth, the impact sending shards of pain into my wrists. I close my eyes and lay there for a few seconds, hoping nothing is broken.

"Jazz? Are you okay?" Lily is kneeling beside me, her hand on my upper back.

I open one eye and try to smile at her. "I'll live," I say. My face burns with embarrassment. Somehow it seems wrong for a Seer to be so completely klutzy.

Ignoring the pain in my wrists, I stand and smooth down the front of the dress. No wonder there were no equal rights for women while they wore clothes like these. I don't know how they ever got anything done.

Lily picks up some small stones. "I think we should try to stay over there," she says, pointing to a row of un-kept rose bushes. "That way we're not easy to spot." I nod, and we quickly run over behind the bushes. Crouching down low, Lily throws a handful of pebbles toward one of the second-storey windows. The tiny rocks make a loud cracking sound as they hit the glass. We both im-mediately lean farther into the bushes. Thorns scratch at my cheeks, and the heavy smell of the roses fills my nostrils, making me feel like sneezing.

"I'm sorry. That was so much louder than I thought it would be," Lily whispers. She presses up beside me, and I can feel her heart beating crazy-fast, like she's just run a marathon. "Do you think the guard heard?"

I shrug my shoulders. I think he'd have to be pretty deaf not to have, but I'm hoping Raphael and Cassandra have him too distracted.

We sit in silence for another couple of seconds. I practically hold my breath until I hear the low murmuring of their conversation. If anything, they seem to have moved even farther away from the house.

Taking a chance, I throw a handful of pebbles at the next window over. They hit the panes of glass and bounce off. The noise is nearly as loud as before.

We wait for a few seconds, carefully watching both windows for any sign of life. I find myself trying not to blink. I'm afraid if I close my eyes for even a second, I'll miss some sign from Jade.

"Are you sure you heard her call your name? From here?" Lily asks, keeping her voice low. The fog is becoming denser and creeping higher.

"Positive. This is where her voice came from, and I saw someone move in the upstairs window, too."

Lily's eyes widen. "But you heard what the guard said. No food or water's been given for over a week. No one can survive that long without water, Jazz."

I shrug. "I just know what I saw and heard. Besides, everyone here is dead, anyway, remember? They don't even need food and water." Irritation bubbles up in my chest. Why is Lily being so negative? I didn't give up on Cassandra in the boat, and that was just a couple of hours ago, so why is she suddenly being all doom and gloom about the possibility of Jade being alive? I try not to think about the fact that Jade, if she actually is not a lost soul, does need water and food to survive....

There's a creaking sound from one of the windows. Lily and I turn our faces toward the noise. The figure at the window is difficult to see, but it's clearly female. Long, dark hair frames the face. I nervously tuck my bottom lip under my front teeth. Is it Jade?

I begin to move from behind the rose bushes, toward the house. Lily grabs me by the arm.

"It's not safe," she says. "We'll know if it's her in a few moments."

The window continues to slowly creak open on its hinges. The fog has thickened around us like a blanket, and is cushioning the sound.

Finally the window swings open, and Jade cautiously leans out. She glances from side to side, checking for the guard. I place two fingers in my mouth and let out a low whistle. Jade looks toward us.

"How are we going to get her down?" Lily asks.

I stand up and turn around. "Unbutton me," I say. Though I have no idea what is under this dress, I do know I'm not wearing panties or a bra.

"What are you going to do?" she asks, her fingers fumbling at the buttons that run the length of the dress. "You can't scale the wall, you know."

I laugh. "Like Spider-Girl? I think I'm pretty special, but not that special. We're going to use the dress to break Jade's fall when she jumps."

As Lily finishes unbuttoning me, I step out of the dress, and stand, shivering, in only a thin, linen smock.

We move closer to the house, glancing around as we do. The fog is now very thick and white. Great for hiding us, but also great for hiding anything that's out to get us, like demons.

"Jasmine? Is that really you?" Jade asks, smiling down at me. She's wearing the same dress I saw in my vision.

"We've come to bring you home," I say, trying to keep my voice as low as possible, which is hard to do because I want to make sure Jade hears me.

A wave of concern washes across her face. I was kind of hoping for relief or joy, but she almost seems troubled that we're planning to take her out of the Place-in-Between. Or maybe I'm just being paranoid.

"We need you to jump," I say. "And then we're going to join the others."

Lily and I hold onto opposite ends of the dress with both hands, pulling the material as tight as possible. It's no substitute for a trampoline, but I hope it will break Jade's fall enough to keep her from getting badly injured. Or killed.

Jade climbs onto the window ledge. She teeters there for a moment, her eyes wide with trepidation. I don't blame her for hesitating. The dress isn't the best way to try and break a two-storey jump, but we don't have a lot of choices.

"Hurry," I say. I glance toward the street. The fog is too thick to see more than a few metres in front of us, and I can't hear Raphael, Cassandra, and the guard talking anymore. Hopefully that just means they've moved even farther away from us.

Jade scrunches up her face, closes her eyes, and leaps.

CHAPTER 21

For a moment she's like an angel suspended in the fog with her arms outstretched, and her dress billowing out around her.

I grasp the fabric of my dress harder, anticipating her impact. We can't let it go, or she'll be badly hurt.

Jade hits the dress less than a second later, and the fabric is pulled violently downward, taking at least four of my fingernails with it. The pain is horrible, but I manage to hang on. Lily lets go with a yelp, but the dress has already done its job. Jade lands safely on the ground with a muted thump.

Bending down, I throw my arms around her shoulders and pull her to me. Tears roll down my cheeks. Jade. She's here. She's alive. We're together.

"I'll never leave you again," I whisper in her ear. "Are you hurt?"

She moans softly and hugs me back.

"I'm okay," she quietly says. "But I don't want to do that again, that's for sure."

Lily squats beside us, holding a finger against her lips. Her eyes are wide with fear. I snap back to reality. We're in danger.

She points at two shadowy figures scurrying, almost soundlessly, over the garden wall.

Slowly and quietly, we inch our way back toward the bushes. "Don't be frightened," I whisper as quietly as I can into Jade's ear. "They won't be able to hurt us if we're not afraid." I actually don't believe that anymore, but figure the less negative emotions the demons — if that's what they are — can feed on, the better.

The three of us move farther into the bushes and watch the two figures walk slowly around the garden in the fog. My bladder feels heavy, but I try to push down any sense of fear I have. Easier said than done.

They're getting closer. Jade sucks in her breath. They stop, as though listening. I swear my heartbeat must be loud enough for them to hear.

One of them moves closer, crouching low to the ground. I feel faint, I'm so terrified now.

"Jazz? Lily?" a voice calls out softly. Cassandra. I press the knuckles of my hand against my mouth to keep from crying out in relief.

"We're over here," Lily replies. She keeps her voice quiet. After all, we don't know who else, or what else, might be out there in the fog.

Raphael and Cassandra make their way over to us.

"Great to meet you, Jade," Raphael says, flashing her one of his charming smiles. "I'm glad we found you safe and sound. Now all we need to do is get out of here as quickly as possible."

That troubled look flickers across Jade's face again. It's just for a second, but it's definite this time. There's something that really bothers her about leaving here.

"What happened to the guard?" I ask Raphael as we walk back to the fence.

"Let's just say I gave him a few shillings to spend at the local pub. It seems he's quite the regular there." Raphael catapults himself over with the ease of an Olympian, his black hair falling forward, temporarily hiding his eyes as he leaps. He lands, and holds out his hand to help Jade down.

I'm next to climb and am extra careful as I navigate the fence. The last thing in the world I want is a replay of my first attempt to get over this stupid thing. I'd die if I tumbled down like that in front of Raphael. So Humpty Dumpty.

We all make it over and stand looking at each other.

"What do we do now?" I ask. "The subway seems to be the way we got here, and the way we can get out. But I don't think there are any subways built yet. Are there?"

Raphael shakes his head. "No, we're about two hundred years too early. But the gateway between worlds has somehow opened. The subway is an easier portal because it's closer to the underworld, to here. But there are other places that will work in much the same way."

"What other places?" Cassandra asks as we begin to walk.

"There's a crypt in Greenwich. It's beneath a church called St. Alfege."

"A crypt?" Lily says. "You mean where they put dead corpses?"

"All corpses are dead, Lily," I say wryly. I give her a good-natured poke in the arm. Not that I like the idea of hanging out with a bunch of rotting bodies either.

I look over at Jade. She's walking beside me in complete silence. I want to ask her what's wrong, but feel that's a question that should be asked in private. After all, I have no idea what she's been through down here, so it's kind of unrealistic and selfish of me to expect her to be completely normal right away.

"It wouldn't be my first choice," Cassandra says with a shrug. "But I'll do anything to get out of here. Especially now that it's nighttime."

The image of Cassandra being dragged away into the crowd, clearly terrified, flashes in my mind. I can't imagine how scared she must've been when they threw her into the water, screaming that she was a witch. No matter how strong a swimmer someone was, these massive dresses would definitely get in the way. Especially once they're wet. I realize I'm still holding mine, and quickly put it back on with help from Cassandra.

Approaching hoof beats on the cobblestones cause all of us to immediately fall silent. We begin to walk with our heads down, watching the ground in front of us. I don't know if this will make us any less recognizable. I get the feeling that the demons don't have to see us to know we're around, anyway. I think they can sense it, or maybe they can even pick up our scent like hunting dogs.

Seconds later, a black horse-drawn carriage emerges out of the mist. It drives straight at us.

Lily screams a warning, and we scatter like bowling pins to either side of the narrow road as the carriage races past. Seconds later, it comes to a halt with a shout and several ear-shattering neighs.

We cautiously walk back toward each other. Obviously, the smartest thing for all of us to do is to keep together; there's safety in numbers.

The horses stamp their hooves impatiently, lift their heads into the air, and neigh again, this time less forcefully. White plumes of misty breath rise from their nostrils. We stop and stand in silence behind the carriage. And we wait.

A few moments later, there's movement from the front of the carriage, and a short man jumps down and walks toward us. He's incredibly muscular, with football player shoulders, and a swagger that makes him seem more pit bull than human. As he gets closer, I notice the determined look on his face.

At least he's not one of *them*.

"Are all of you looking to be flattened, or are ye looking for a ride?" he asks, holding the lantern he's carrying up to get a better look at us. His voice is a low, pleasant rumble, like distant thunder on a hazy summer's afternoon.

I turn to Raphael.

"It's okay," he says, keeping his voice low. "He's just a lost soul. He may have been a bus or taxi driver when he was alive, so he still wants to take people where they need to go."

Sadness sweeps over me. I can't imagine what it would be like to be stuck in time, forever doing the same thing.

"A ride," Jade says to the man, interrupting my thoughts. "To Greenwich, please." We all turn our heads and stare at her in surprise. "What?" she asks. "Isn't that where we want to go?"

There's a murmur of agreement as we follow the driver. He saunters back to the carriage and opens the door for us.

"Your carriage awaits," he says, a big, toothy grin spreading across his face.

The ride to Greenwich is eerily quiet. Other than the steady pounding of the horses' hooves against the road, the fog continues to blanket us in silence. I peer out the carriage window, but am unable to see farther than a few centimetres because of the thick, white mist. I like that it is hiding us from whatever is lurking out there in the darkness. But it's a double-edged sword: we could be taken by complete surprise by the demons as well.

Jade squeezes my hand. "I don't know if I can leave here," she whispers. Her eyebrows draw tightly together with worry.

I squeeze her hand in return. "We're together now. You'll be okay. Raphael has a way of keeping everyone around him … safe." I think about Cassandra floating limply in the water. Okay, it's a tiny lie, but I figure it is better than saying he has a way of bringing people back from the brink of death. The less she knows of what we've faced to get to her, the better.

Jade shakes her head.

"It's not that," she says. "You're going to think I'm crazy, but it's like there's something … missing. It happened when they first brought me here. Part of me …" She stops and looks over at the others. "Feels empty now. Dead."

"What do you mean?" I ask. "Maybe it's just because we were apart?"

"I don't think so…. It's hard to explain." She bites her bottom lip nervously. "Something happened a few days ago, and then I felt better. More real. It was just for a few seconds, but since then, I've been able to see you. And to remember who I was … am."

The others are listening now.

"The gateway," Raphael says. "Maybe that's when it opened."

"When I first saw you, Jazz," Jade whispers, "I think you were in a kitchen. There were cupboards and stuff behind you. I only saw you for a couple of seconds, but it made me remember that I am a twin and that I had another life before all of this." She makes a sweeping motion with her hand. "Does that make any sense? Or do I just sound crazy?"

"Everything that's been happening to us is crazy," Cassandra says. "Welcome to our little club of insanity."

And then I remember. Lola's doll. When I'd picked it up in the kitchen, I saw Jade screaming for help.

"No," I say, trying to swallow down the lump of fear rising in my throat. "It doesn't sound crazy at all because I remember seeing you here, too. It happened when I picked up this wooden doll of Lola's a few days ago. And I was in the kitchen when I found it."

We stare at each other for a moment.

"Where is that doll now?" Jade whispers. Her voice quivers.

I shrug my shoulders. "Lola took it back. Why do you think we were able to see each other through it?"

She looks hard at me. "I don't know, but when you touched it, for a few seconds, I felt alive again."

I don't dare tell her that I dropped the doll because I felt that holding on to it, for even a moment longer, would kill me.

CHAPTER 22

About half an hour later, the carriage stops. It's pitch black outside. I can't help but wonder how the horses were able to keep to the road with only the driver's lanterns to guide them.

"St. Alfege awaits," our driver says, opening the door. All of us look exhausted, except for Raphael and Jade. "You'll want to mind yourselves out here at night. Souls less savoury than yours take refuge in the dark."

"No kidding," I say, lifting my skirts to hop out of the carriage. The driver holds out his hand for me. I reach for it and feel his cold, jelly-like flesh. A shiver runs through me. Everything seems so real here, it's sometimes hard to remember that everyone, and everything, is dead. Or at least would be dead on Earth.

"Here," the driver says to Cassandra after she's leapt to the ground. "You'll need light of some sort once I'm gone." He hands her a lantern. Inside the thick glass, a candle flickers.

Once Raphael jumps out, the driver closes the carriage door and hops back onto his seat. The horses paw nervously at the ground, as if eager to get away. I wonder how animals end up down here and make a mental note to ask Raphael about that later.

"Best of luck and may ye stay safe," the driver says. He tips his cap at us and then snaps his leather whip against the horses' flanks. The carriage pulls away, leaving us in the fog. St. Alfege looms in front of us.

"What now?" Lily asks. Dark circles frame her eyes.

We all gaze at each other. The candlelight is barely bright enough to illuminate our faces. Darkness presses in around us. The night air feels alive; it's pulsating like a heart. I want to get inside and away from it, but know that what waits for us in the crypt might be much worse.

"I think we need to get inside the church," Cassandra says, turning on her heel. Lily and Jade quickly follow. Clearly, they're sensing something in the darkness as well.

Raphael falls into step beside me.

"How come you never mentioned the doll?" he asks.

I shrug my shoulders. "Why would I? I didn't even know you when it happened. It was a random thing."

"That's just it, Jazz. I don't think it was random at all. You said the doll belongs to a woman named Lola?"

"Yeah. She's my mom's best friend. We've known her since we were born." It feels unbelievably great to be able to speak about me and Jade as a unit again.

"I know who Lola is," he says as we walk into the churchyard.

Cassandra pauses and shines the dim light of the lantern at the stone posts that loom out of the darkness on either side of the stone gateway into the churchyard. I look away from the carved faces peering out at me. They're tiny cherubs, the kind you see on Valentine's Day cards, but these ones look incredibly sad.

"How do you know who Lola is?" I ask. "Did you run into her in our building or something?"

"Remember I said that all Seers have Protectors?"

"Yeah …" Where's he going with this?

He slows his pace, allowing the others to move slightly ahead of us. They're climbing the steps to the church. A finger of cold traces its way along the length of my spine. I don't want to be left out here in the darkness, even if Raphael is with me.

"Lola was a Protector. She was supposed to be looking out for you and Jade."

I stop. "Lola? Are you telling me she knows all about this Seer stuff?"

There's a loud creaking sound as the heavy wooden doors to the church open like a dark mouth. I stifle the urge to scream at Cassandra, Lily, and Jade to stop. Suddenly the church seems like a bad idea. But then what would we do to get back to modern-day Toronto?

"You need to tell me how Lola is involved in all of this," I say, sweeping my arms in front of me. "This nightmare."

"We lost contact with her shortly after Jade's abduction. Lola told us she was certain Jade was dead, that she felt she'd failed her, and wanted to relinquish her role as a Protector."

"Well, she did think Jade was dead," I say. "We all did. Lola was part of the search parties that looked for my sister for nearly a month."

We've reached the entrance of the church. Lily is waiting for us, propping the door open with her body.

"This place is really creepy," she says. Cassandra stands behind her with Jade. They both look like they haven't slept in days.

"You look exhausted, Jasmine," Cassandra says, bringing the lantern closer to my face. "Are you feeling okay?"

"I was going to say the same thing about you," I retort.

Raphael frowns. "You all look tired because you're not supposed to be down here this long. The Place-in-Between is for the dead, not the living. We need to get you home soon."

"How is being in here going to help us get back?" Lily asks. Panic edges her words. "There are dead people all over the place. We're in death central."

And that's when we hear it: the sound of something dragging against the stone floor.

We fall silent. I want to tell Cassandra to blow out the candle in her lantern, so that if anything is in here with us, we're not visible. The problem being, if we do that, we'll be in complete darkness with whatever is moving around in here.

Then we hear footsteps. Not heavy, clunking zombie footsteps, but scurrying, light footsteps. The sound a bunch of mice running along a cement floor might make. Except these would have to be giant, mutant mice.

"Oh, my God. Oh, my God. Oh, my God," Lily says. She gulps at the air like a goldfish that's jumped out of its bowl. I'm afraid she's going to hyperventilate.

"Calm down," Raphael says. "You'll make it worse by being this afraid."

"He's right," I whisper, grabbing her arm. "They become stronger from our negative emotions, remember? Anyway, we've got strength in numbers." I say this, even though I don't believe we can fight a bunch of demons right now. I feel completely drained.

But Lily doesn't even seem to notice me. "I want to go home. Now," she whimpers, her voice rising. She's staring into the darkness, her eyes wild with panic and fear. "I want to be in Toronto. I want to be at home in my bed. I don't believe all of this." She's practically shouting now, and despite me trying to keep my own emotions down, I find myself growing more scared by the second.

"This has got to be a bad dream!" she screeches, grabbing her head in her hands.

And that's when Jade begins to scream.

"Something's got me!" she shrieks. The terror in her voice makes my entire body go cold.

I rush to help her, but am seconds too late. Jade is pulled face down to the floor of the church by a figure cloaked in a hooded garment. This demon is fast. Jade's arms pinwheel in the air as she drops. One of her hands knocks the lantern Cassandra's holding, and it falls to the ground with a crashing thud. The candle flickers inside the smashed glass for a moment before going out.

We're in pitch darkness. Lily begins to scream in unison with Jade.

"I hate this! This is a place for dead people. I want to be home in Toronto!"

I'm on the floor as she shrieks, desperately trying to locate Jade. I can hear her, but when I reach for out in the direction of her voice, my fingers just keep finding the hard, stone floor of the church. I move forward as quickly as I can. Whatever grabbed her, it's dragging her away from us, toward the front of the church. Toward where Raphael said the entrance to the crypt is located.

I rush forward on my hands, scrabbling along the floor like a crab, praying nothing grabs me as well. Jade is not going to be taken away from me again. I'm not going to let this happen.

Suddenly, the floor drops away from underneath me, and I'm falling into what seems like a very deep hole. As the air rushes past me, I realize everything is silent. I can't hear Lily or Jade or anybody anymore. I close my eyes (which is kind of funny because I can't see anything in the inky blackness anyhow) and brace for a crash landing.

CHAPTER 23

There's screaming all around me again. I've landed on a hard surface, but not nearly as hard as I'd expected, considering I must've fallen at least three storeys from the church floor.

I open my eyes. Someone is shining a light in my face. I smell smoke mingled with some sort of sweet, coppery scent, and I can just make out the faint outline of twisted metal and seat cushions. The air is thick with smoke and dust from the debris.

"Are you okay?" the person with the flashlight asks. I nod. She's wearing a Toronto Police uniform. It seems I'm back. No more demons.

"Where's my sister?" I ask. "Her name is Jade. Have you seen her?" I sit up. Other than a dull, throbbing ache at my right hip, I feel fine.

"I don't think so. But we're just getting to people now. Are you in any pain?"

I shake my head. "What happened?"

The officer's lips tighten. "We're not 100 percent sure, but it seems that some sort of explosion occurred in the subway car in front of this one."

My eyes widen. "You mean a bomb?"

"It's too soon to speculate," she quickly says. "And it wouldn't help anyone in here to think that right now. What's your name?"

"Jasmine," I reply. "Jasmine Guzman."

"Okay, Jasmine," the officer says. "We're going to get you out of here as soon as we can. We just need to move some of the more seriously injured passengers that need immediate medical attention first. You're sure you're not in a lot of pain?"

I nod. "I'm sure."

"Then I'll be back as soon as I can," she says. "I'm Officer Riley, by the way."

"Okay. I'll be here," I say, shooting her a wry smile.

Officer Riley turns and begins to make her way farther down the carriage, the beam of her flashlight casting eerie shadows around the mangled wreckage of the subway train. I can hear faint moaning coming from different places, including the shattered car in front of us.

"Jazz, is that you?" a voice whispers weakly from behind me.

I look over my shoulder. Cassandra is lying within arm's reach, near one of the subway doors.

"Yeah, it's me," I say, moving toward her. I carefully crawl over bits of twisted metal and torn seat cushions, hoping there are no body parts in the debris.

"I think I blacked out for a minute," she says, propping herself up onto her elbows. Blood trickles down the side of her face from a gash on her left temple. It doesn't look very deep, so I hope there's nothing to worry about.

"Are you okay?" I ask, kneeling beside her.

She coughs a bit and sits up. "I think so. What happened?"

"There's been an accident. One of the police officers said it was an explosion or something."

Cassandra's eyes widen. "We're back in Toronto, right?"

I nod. "As far as I can tell."

"Where are the others?" she asks, looking around. "Is Lily okay?"

The beam from Officer Riley's flashlight approaches. There's a paramedic with her who introduces herself as Samantha and starts to examine Cassandra's injuries.

"Jasmine? We've found your sister," she says, stopping and squatting beside Cassandra and me. "She's going to be fine. She has no significant injuries, aside from a nasty ankle wound. We're getting her out on a stretcher right now. There are emergency personnel at ground level that will be seeing to her and transporting her to the nearest hospital."

"My sister is on here, as well. I think," Cassandra interjects. "Her name is Lily."

"We haven't come across her yet," Officer Riley says. "But I understand that about a half-dozen other passengers were already escorted out. They're at ground level. As soon as Samantha's cleaned out that wound on your head, you two can come with me, and we'll have you join them."

A few minutes later, we follow Officer Riley out of the train and onto the tracks.

"Can't we get electrocuted doing this?" Cassandra asks.

"The power's been cut," Officer Riley answers. "No subway cars are running until we find out exactly what's happened here."

The tunnel is eerie and filled with the moaning cries of the injured passengers still trapped and being treated in the wreckage. I'm super glad when we finally reach the platform, and two firefighters pull us up into the station. I just want to be above ground, among the living. And I want to find Jade.

Officer Riley leaves us with the firefighters, who walk us up the escalators and outside.

The bright sunshine hurts my eyes, forcing me to squint, as we emerge out of the station and onto the sidewalk. The heat hits me like a slap. I'm not used to it — the Place-in-Between was so much cooler.

"Oh, my God," Cassandra says.

There are paramedics and emergency workers rushing all around us. Journalists buzz about the periphery of the area like bees, and the sound of helicopters and drones fills the air above our heads. The area is completely blocked off, but loads of people are gathering behind the police lines, trying to see what's happening. Injured passengers from the subway are everywhere.

One middle-aged woman is slumped up against the glass wall of a bus stop; the white bandage wrapped around her head is turning a deep crimson. A paramedic holds a water bottle to her lips. I notice she's missing a shoe. Her other foot is bloody but still fastened inside an expensive-looking, black, high-heeled sandal.

Cassandra sucks in her breath. "There's Lily!" she says, pointing toward a line of stretchers near some ambulances. I look over and see Lily crouching beside one of the stretchers.

We run over. Jade's on the stretcher beside Lily. She's propped up on her elbows, talking to Lily and the paramedic assisting her, so I know she can't be too badly injured. I breathe a sigh of relief.

Lily lets out an elated squeal as soon as she sees us and throws herself at Cassandra.

"I'm so glad you're okay," she says. "What happened back there?"

"I don't know," I answer. "But if those guys are here, I'm guessing it's something pretty bad." I nod my head toward a group of heavily armed police officers in riot gear entering the subway station.

"Climate-change terrorists strike again," Cassandra says, her voice grim.

I walk over to Jade, lean in, and kiss her on the cheek. "How does it feel to be back?" I whisper.

"Painful," she says. "My ankle is shredded. Whatever grabbed me down there in the church had some mean claws."

I straighten and glance over at the paramedic to see if she overheard. "It's better if we talk about things like that at home," I say. "And, speaking of home, Mom is going to die when she sees you."

"Sorry to interrupt, girls, but we've got to take her to the hospital now to get her leg looked at," the paramedic says, fastening the straps of the stretcher around Jade's midsection. "Do you want to come with us? You can give your mom a call from the ambulance."

I pause. How can I just call Mom up and announce that her missing, and presumed dead, daughter is suddenly back?

"My mom usually turns off her phone in the afternoon because she works nights and, um, has to sleep," I say. "So … I'll have to run back home and come to the hospital with her. Since she'll have to wake up and everything."

"We'll go with Jade in the ambulance," Cassandra says. She turns to the paramedic. "If that's okay?"

The paramedic nods. "You can sit up front." As she climbs into the back, she turns to me, "Let your mom know we're taking your sister to Sick Kids."

"Okay. See you soon," I say as Jade's stretcher is hoisted into the air. I turn, trying to figure out how to get out of here, and get home as quickly as possible.

Just as I'm squeezing past the police barricades, I realize something. Raphael's nowhere to be found. And the weirdest thing is, I didn't even think about him until right now. It's like I forgot he was ever with us.

CHAPTER 24

The front door of our apartment looms in front of me. I stand in the hall outside, listening to a lonely dog whimpering in another apartment and taking in the odour of fried onions and stale smoke.

What am I going to say when I see Mom? How do I possibly explain Jade being back, or how I found her? Do I say I just bumped into her at the Eaton Centre?

Suddenly, I realize I've been away all night without even calling. Mom must be worried sick.

Bracing myself for her reaction, I open the door and walk straight to the living room.

Bright beams of sunlight flood the room. The worn Persian rug is rolled into one corner, and the coffee table nearly trips me up. Mom's doing yoga in a space she's cleared in front of the video monitor. She shoots me an upside-down smile and slowly lifts herself out of downward dog.

"*Hola*, baby girl," she says, coming over and giving me a massive kiss on both cheeks. "How was your sleepover with your friends?"

I look at her blankly. The last time she saw me, the sun was nearly setting.

"Hello?" Mom laughs. "Anyone there? Cassandra's mother is nice, no? We spoke for a bit when she called asking if you could stay there last night."

I have no idea what she's talking about, but clearly she's not upset about me being gone all night. And this isn't the time to get into all of that anyhow. Right now I need to tell Mom about Jade being back without giving her a heart attack.

"I … I need you to sit down," I stammer. My hands are shaking, so I fold them behind my back. "There's something I have to tell you."

Mom's eyes narrow. "You in trouble, *pobrecita*?" She wipes away the beads of sweat on her forehead with a pink hand towel.

I shake my head. "No. It's good news. Great news, in fact. It's just …"

"Just what?" She's getting impatient, making the words stick in my throat like peanut butter.

"Jade's alive," I say.

Mom stares hard at me, her eyes filling with tears. "What do you mean? Are you seeing things again, *mija*?" she asks.

Well, yeah, I think. *I have been seeing demons again, except now I know they're real. And they're capable of some very serious damage, like kidnapping little girls called Seers and holding them hostage in Limbo….*

"I can't explain everything right now," I say. "But she's at Sick Kid's waiting for you."

Mom blesses herself and begins crying openly. I haven't seen her do this since Jade's disappearance.

"Are you lying to me, Jasmine Alejandra? Or have the angels finally answered my prayers?" she asks, coming over and placing her hands on both my shoulders. Tears are streaming down her cheeks. "Is this a dream?"

"You're not dreaming and I'm not lying," I say. "Come on, we need to get over there. Cassandra and Lily are with her."

Mom rushes to her room and returns seconds later with a long, white button-down shirt thrown over her yoga tights. Her face is flushed, and she dabs at her eyes with a tissue.

"I've become such an old woman since my baby was stolen," she says wistfully. "What will she think of me? So much time has passed. Did you get to speak with her? Is she hurt? Why is she at the hospital? *Where has she been?*"

The questions are making me dizzy. I need to be careful here, not only about what I say, but also to remember whatever stories I tell her in the next few minutes. If I can't tell Mom the truth, the least I can do is keep my lies straight.

"We really need to go," I say again. "The streetcar is going to be packed. There was some sort of an accident on the subway."

Mom picks up her phone. "Then I'll just call Lola to take us."

My heart skips a beat. Lola. She was our Protector. Except, for some reason, she wasn't able to protect Jade from the demon that took her.

But I believe Raphael thinks there's more to it than that. I know he wanted to tell me more before we entered the church, but didn't have the time. And I want to find out the rest of the story before Lola discovers that Jade's back.

"We shouldn't bother her," I say. "The streetcars won't be that bad. I'm sure they've got things cleared up. The drones will be reporting back about traffic by the second."

Mom stares at me. "If there's been an accident, it will be a nightmare, no matter what. You know that."

If I continue arguing, Mom will suspect something's up.

It doesn't matter anyway. She's already on the phone, and within fifteen minutes we're crammed into Lola's car, heading toward the hospital. Traffic is bumper-to-bumper; the cars ahead of us crawl along like ants heading to a picnic.

Lola leans over the steering wheel, her face partially hidden by the biggest pair of sunglasses I've ever seen.

"Tell me this again," she says. "Jade is alive? Are you sure?"

"Yep," I reply. I glance out the window and watch a group of cyclists pass us, their noses and mouths covered with masks to filter out the pollution. Even though Lola's car runs on electricity, I feel guilty being in it. After all, batteries aren't exactly carbon neutral. We've never even owned a car, though that's mostly because they cost too much money these days. I've never thought to ask how Lola affords hers.

"But that's impossible," she replies. "Jade's dead."

"Technically, it's not impossible," I say. "Her body was never found. The police and everyone just assumed she was dead."

Mom nods. "I never told either of you this, but I always felt, down deep in my heart, that Jade was alive. Remember that girl ... what was her name? The one that was taken from her family's holiday home in Spain when she was three?"

"Jolene Smart?" Lola asks.

"That's the one," Mom says with a wistful smile. "They found her after fifteen years, remember? She was living with a family in America who'd made her believe that she was really their daughter. Fifteen years. I'm sure most people believed she was dead, too."

"But Jade's case is different," Lola interjects. I notice she's gripping the steering wheel more tightly now. We make a sharp turn into the parking lot for the hospital.

"How is it different?" I ask as the car slides into a parking spot.

Lola turns off the ignition and shrugs. "I just feel it is."

We enter the hospital, passing its three-dimensional plasma images of famous cartoon animals and brightly coloured butterflies that move toward us, large smiles plastered across their faces. The hospital is obviously attempting to make the space as welcoming and child-friendly as possible, yet this still has to be the single most depressing place on Earth. A young boy without any hair shuffles past me in slipper-clad feet, his father walking beside him, rolling a pole with a clear IV bag hanging from it. I smile at the boy, even though the sight of him makes me want to cry. He beams a toothy grin back at me.

Mom rushes up to the information desk. Lola is right behind her. I might be imagining things, but Lola looks very uncomfortable, like she's constipated and confused all at once. But maybe I'm just reading into it, and she actually just feels like me — uneasy in a place where so many kids are suffering.

"My baby is here," Mom says. Her accent always thickens when she's emotional. "Her name is Jade Guzman."

This is so surreal. I pinch myself hard on the bicep to make sure I'm not dreaming. Jade is here....

The nurse looks over her blue-rimmed glasses at Mom. "Is she your daughter?"

Mom nods. Tears are sliding down her cheeks again. I walk over, take her hand, and squeeze it hard.

"Jade's my twin sister," I say. "The paramedics are expecting us. We were on the subway this afternoon when the accident happened."

The nurse frowns. "The police are questioning some of the injured at the moment. They'll want to speak with you as well."

"The police?" Mom asks, shocked. "Why do the police need to question my girls?"

"It's already been leaked to the media, so I guess we're okay to tell you," the nurse says. "Apparently, the accident on the subway today was no accident. It was a bombing. The police suspect climate-change terrorists."

My heart skips a beat. "Was anyone killed?" I ask.

The nurse looks at me. "Not that we know of, but several passengers are listed in critical condition."

I swallow hard. "Has a boy named Raphael been admitted here?" I ask. The pounding of my heart fills my head. "He's fourteen or fifteen."

"Last name?" the nurse asks.

"I don't know," I say. "But he's my friend. He was with us in the subway."

The nurse looks at her computer screen. I hold my breath, waiting for her answer.

"No one by that name was admitted here. He could've been taken to another hospital, though we were asked to take all the under-eighteens. Maybe he's okay?" she says.

Maybe, I think. *Hopefully.*

Suddenly, a man runs up to us and sticks a microphone in Mom's face. "Ms. Guzman, can you tell us where your daughter's been for the last four years?"

"What was she doing on the subway today? Was she injured in the explosion?" another reporter calls out.

Flashes of light explode in front of my face as we dodge cameras and news drones on our way to Jade's room. Two hospital security guards, with bodies more ape than human, are assigned to help us.

"Don't say anything yet," one of them cautions us, his blue eyes narrowing at a female journalist that jumps in front of us like a ninja. He sticks his arm out, palm forward, warning her to back away.

I look over at Mom. He needn't worry. She's speechless. Tears of joy wet her cheeks as she rushes into the hospital room. The security guards quickly close the door as several journalists, the cameras on the drones above their heads clicking away, attempt to follow us.

"*Gloria a Dios!*" Mom cries, rushing to the bed and throwing her arms around Jade's neck.

Lola stands to one side of the bed and watches, her face devoid of emotion, as Mom and Jade embrace, both of them sobbing openly now.

I stare at Lola until I catch her eye. Then I raise an eyebrow. Why isn't she happier to see Jade?

She quickly looks away and out the windows, pretending to stare hard at something beyond the fringe of trees on the other side of the glass.

"*Mi nena!* My angel!" Mom exclaims, tears streaming down her face. Strands of tear-soaked hair stick to her cheeks. Brushing them away, she sits back and stares at Jade.

"Is this real?" she whispers to no one in particular, clutching at a tissue with her hand. "Am I dreaming?"

I rush over and hug her. "It's real." Reaching out, I take one of Jade's hands in mine. She shoots me a weak smile.

Even the two security guards flanking the door appear to be getting a bit emotional. I notice one of them clear his throat self-consciously and dab at the corner of his eyes.

Mom grabs Jade's other hand. "Who took you? How did you escape? What did they …" She stops talking, her face crumpling with emotion like a week old jack-o'-lantern. "What did they do to you when they had you? Did they hurt you?"

Jade glances at me. Panic washes over her face.

"It's okay if you can't remember," I say.

Jade nods. "I don't know who took me," she says. "It's weird. I can't tell you anything about what happened from the day I was taken to now."

I smile. My sister hates lying, especially to Mom. This is her way of getting around that. When you think about it — she really can't tell Mom what happened. It's too unbelievable. Talking about demons, the Place-in-Between, and time-travelling through London would mean a one-way ticket to the psych ward. Guaranteed.

"Perhaps that is for the best," Mom says, leaning over and kissing Jade's cheek. "All that matters is that I have both my girls with me again. Now everything will be okay."

CHAPTER 25

"Something's not right," Jade whispers to me as soon as Mom leaves our bedroom.

She's lying against the pillow, her dark hair framing her pale face.

"What do you mean?" I ask. Of course things aren't going to seem right to her. She's been gone for so many years, and so much has changed. I think of how much worse things would've seemed if Mom was still sick.

"I don't feel right. It's as if …" she pauses, her eyes widening. "As if I'm getting weaker and weaker every minute I'm here."

"You're probably just in shock or something," I say, glancing toward the open doorway. Mom's gone to get some juice and soup. I don't want her overhearing any of this.

I sit down on the edge of the bed and take Jade's hand. Her skin feels clammy and cold against mine.

"Your injuries aren't bad," I say, trying to reassure her. "Being back is going to feel weird, that's all. There's going to be an adjustment period. And all the crazy media camping on our doorstep isn't going to make that any easier."

Jade shakes her head. "No, that's not it," she says. "And it has nothing to do with my ankle or what happened on the subway … or even the journalists. I've felt this way from the second I returned. I feel like I'm draining away."

"You're tired. You've been through a lot."

She pauses. "You need to listen to me, Jazz. I think I'm dying," she whispers.

"How are my girls?" Mom asks, entering the room with a tray of steaming soup. She sets it down on the bedside table and hands me a bowl. "Chicken noodle. You both need something to nourish you after what's happened."

"Thanks," I say. The bowl's warmth is a startling contrast to the chill of Jade's hand.

Mom perches on the edge of the bed and holds a bowl for Jade to take sips from.

I watch my sister carefully drink from the lip of the white bowl. She looks incredibly fragile, almost like a baby bird, with her head bobbing unsteadily as she sips at the broth. Dark, purplish circles frame her eyes.

My appetite deserts me. I put down my soup bowl and walk over to the window.

The street below is buzzing with activity: television vans, news drones, and reporters crowd the street in front of the house. They look uncomfortable in the noonday sun. Another heat and energy advisory is in effect for today, with the temperature climbing to the high forties again.

I wonder if climate-change terrorists really did blow up our subway train, or if we somehow caused the explosion when we came back from the Place-in-Between. The timing seems too coincidental.

And I still haven't heard from Raphael. My texts and calls remain unanswered.

"Lola thinks we should leave Toronto," Mom says abruptly.

I turn back around. "Why?"

"She says things are going to get worse. That the subway bombing is just the beginning of a possible wave of terrorism. And I think that we're all going to need a break from the media circus out there," she says, cocking her head toward the bedroom window.

"I don't think the terrorism is going to get that bad," I say. "Canada's one of the only countries still letting in climate-change refugees. Other places will be targeted first."

Jade's watching us intently. Confusion flits across her face, and I realize she has practically no idea what we're talking about. Of course we learned about climate change and the early climate-change wars in school, but things weren't nearly as bad before she disappeared as they are now.

"Immigration will be stopped soon enough," Mom says. "Too many people are heading here. We don't have enough resources. Especially water. The government is debating an emergency bill to close the borders as we speak. Look at Los Angeles. No one can live there anymore."

I think about the African twins whose mother enrolled them at Beaconsfield the other day. Their mother was so grateful to be here, to be safe.

"How do you know too many people are coming here? Who gets to decide we're not sharing resources?" I ask.

My mother raises an eyebrow as a warning that I need to watch the way I'm saying things to her.

"Femi told Lola that many ships are on their way. Ships from Africa, Asia, and even as far away as Australia."

Lola's son, Femi, works in Ottawa for the government. I'm not sure what he does, but it has something to do with the environment and climate-change immigration. He's only in his early twenties, so it's amazing he's got such an important position so soon out of university.

"So what are we going to do? Turn people away? Send them back to die in droughts and wars?" I ask.

Mom doesn't say anything. Instead, she turns and continues to feed Jade the remainder of her soup.

"Seriously. This is screwed up. And where exactly does Lola expect us to go?"

"She thinks we should head to the countryside. Out of the city. A woman she knows is okay with us staying at her cottage for a few months. And she brings up a good point: it will be a more positive place for Jade. We'll be away from the city, and around nature. The media are going to continue crawling all over us until a more exciting story breaks."

"A few *months*?"

"Do this for your sister, Jasmine. I realize it won't be easy for you."

I look over at Jade. She's pale, and her eyes keep closing as she watches us talk. There *is* something wrong with her. I can feel it. She's slipping away. Maybe being out of the city and away from the reporters knocking at our door will be the best thing for her. Except that means I'll be away from Beaconsfield and our Protectors as well. And Raphael. If Raphael is still around....

"When does Lola want us to leave?"

Mom grimaces and I dread what she's about to say before the words are even out of her mouth. And that's because I've just read her mind. Her thoughts are filling my head. My powers as a Seer seem to be stronger now that Jade is here.

"Tomorrow. Lola's arranged to pick us up early in the morning. I'll call your school and let them know you'll be away for awhile." She watches me, waiting for my reaction.

"Fine," I say. "I'll go, but I'm not saying I'll stay for *months*. In fact, I'm not committing to anything, but ..." I look over at Jade again. She's asleep. If it weren't for the shallow rise and fall of her chest, it would be easy to believe she was dead. "It probably is good for Jade to recover in a place that is more peaceful and quiet."

I'm about to fall asleep that night, suitcases packed beside my bed, when something hits the window. It's almost like a hard tap. The second time I hear the sound, I sit up and look around, my eyes slowly adjusting to the shadowy light of my bedroom.

Jade's asleep, only a few metres away, on the futon. Though it's reassuring that she's so close, her breath is now shallow and raspy, as if she has pneumonia. Her condition is getting worse for sure.

Something hits the window again. I swing my legs over the side of the bed and slip my feet into my slippers before shuffling over and putting my forehead against the glass of the windowpane. I peer out into the darkness. We keep the windows closed and the air conditioning on low because it's still so hot at night.

Someone, or something is crouching in the upper branches of the trees just outside my window. I jump back, startled. My heart feels like it might jump out of my mouth, but then I realize that I'm back in Toronto, and whatever's in the tree most likely isn't demonic. Though a having a human lurking about, looking into my bedroom window at night is not much better.

I move back to the window and cup my hands on either side of my eyes in order to get a better look. It takes a second to adjust to the darkness. Raphael waves to me from one of the branches.

Hands shaking, I slide the window open. The screen prevents me from sticking my head out. Raphael puts an index finger to his lips.

"Meet me out front," he says.

I nod, close the window, quickly throw on a pair of jeans and a tank top, and tiptoe through the apartment to the front door. Mom would kill me if she knew I was sneaking out at one in the morning.

Raphael's already leaning against the thick trunk of the tree by the time I get outside. He smiles that lopsided grin of his at me, and for a moment, I melt like butter. But then I remember how he left all of us during the subway accident, and I march over to him.

"Where have you been? Thanks for taking off and leaving us on a bombed subway. And why haven't you answered my calls? My texts?"

His expression remains calm. "You don't understand, Jazz."

"Like hell I don't understand," I shout. "You left us. I might've been dead for all you knew." Anger rises in me. I haven't felt this way in a while. I shove Raphael hard in the chest.

"Don't you care about me at all?" Tears well up in my eyes. Great. Now he knows exactly how I feel about him.

Raphael grabs me by the wrists. Hard.

"Listen to me, Jazz," he says, leaning in close. "Of course I do. I care about you a great deal. That's why I wasn't on the train. I knew you were okay. But other things are happening. Terrible things."

I stare at him. "Like what?"

"Demons are on this side. They're here and there are greater numbers of them every day. I don't know if they got through with us, or if darker forces are at work. Either way, you're not safe. No Seers or their Protectors are safe now."

Despite the heat, a shiver runs through me. "What about Jade? For your information, she's anything but okay."

"That's what I came to talk to you about," Raphael says, letting go of my wrists. "The doll. The one you said you touched just before you had the vision of Jade. What did it look like?"

"I don't know. It was wooden, and it looked African. Maybe like something from Nigeria, where Lola's from."

Raphael frowns. "I need you to listen really carefully, Jazz, because I'm not going to be around in the next little while to guard you or guide you."

"You're taking off again?" I say, shoving him in the chest once more. Though it's meant to be a playful shove, it comes off a little harder. I can't help it; the fact that he's leaving just reinforces the fact that he obviously isn't that into me. "Where are you going now?"

"My brothers need me," Raphael says. He's calm and unflustered; it's as if the shove hasn't happened at all. "I don't have much time. You have to get that doll and destroy it. Look up 'Ibeji' tonight, before you leave the city."

"How do you know I'm leaving the city?" I ask, narrowing my eyes at him. I glance up at the tree. "And how could you have possibly climbed to the top of that tree, and then back down so fast? It's not humanly possible."

"I can't explain it to you it," Raphael says. "I wish I could. Believe me, Jazz. I wish I could." He leans in close, his black hair falling forward across his forehead. For a moment he just stares into my eyes. "You just need to be very careful when you are away from here."

And that's when I realize he wants to kiss me. His thought plays in my mind as clearly as a television show.

I move forward and quickly kiss him. His lips are warm and soft and then —

It's just like what happened when I touched Lola's doll; I begin to see things. Except this time a tsunami of horrific images comes crashing into my mind, all jumbled up and confused. There are awful, terrible visions of human beings being tortured, raped, and burned. Screams fill my head. I see battles and people dying and bodies thrown in heaps like garbage. Men on horses ride into burning villages, hacking at the people with machetes, grabbing children....

I pull away from Raphael — or he pushes me. I can't really tell which because my my body is numb, paralyzed. My head feels like it's been pounded against a brick wall, over and over. Everything is spinning. I look up into the tree, and for a moment, I swear the branches are moving toward me like predatory snakes.

Then Raphael is holding me. I think he's actually holding me up because I can't feel my legs. A few lights flicker on in our apartment building. Someone pokes his head out of one of the lower windows.

"Keep it down out there, will you? Some of us are trying to sleep, ya bunch of hooligans!"

Raphael steers me deeper into the shadow of the tree.

"You just screamed," he whispers. "Hopefully your mom and Jade don't wake up and notice you're gone."

I stare at him, not fully trusting myself to speak. He pulls me close, and I feel the warmth of his chest against mine.

"What are you?" I finally ask. My voice is hoarse.

Raphael doesn't say anything. I wonder if he's even heard me. There are dogs barking in the yard behind my apartment building.

"What are you?" I repeat, turning my face away from his chest to look him in the eye. He suddenly seems incredibly sad.

"This should never have happened, Jazz," he says.

"Why?" I ask.

"Because I'm an angel."

CHAPTER 26

My eyes won't stay open no matter what I do. Pinching myself really hard on the fleshy part of my upper arm doesn't help. Neither does holding my breath until I'm about to pass out. Finally, I give in and fall asleep for a few brief moments, until my head jerks back up as though I am a puppet on a string.

Mom notices my sudden movement and turns to look over her shoulder at me. She's in the front seat of the car beside Lola.

"You look so tired," she says with a frown. "Did you not sleep well last night?"

Understatement of the year, I think. I nod. "Bad dreams."

"Then let yourself nap a bit," she says with a smile. "Though you'll have plenty of time to do that in cottage country. Peace and quiet for my two girls."

I grimace. She has no idea the danger we're in. Napping is not an option.

Last night, after Raphael left, I snuck back into the apartment, still feeling shocked and weak from the nightmarish images I'd seen, and his confession about being an angel. Though the thinking part of my brain said he was completely nuts, after all I'd been through to get Jade back, my heart didn't doubt him for a second when he told me about being an angel. He also warned me to not fully trust Lola. It was hard to hear, but the reality I thought was my life for the last fourteen years is clearly no longer true. The only thing I know for certain these days is that my mind needs to be open and alert to the danger around me.

I knew I wouldn't be able to sleep until I'd looked up Ibeji dolls, so I grabbed my tablet, curled up on the sofa with a blanket and began to search.

Loads of sites came up. I clicked on the first link and began reading:

> The Ibeji doll is of great significance to the Yoruba people of Nigeria. The dolls represent the cult of twin worship. The rate of twin births in the Yoruba is extremely high; approximately forty-five out of every one thousand births are twins.
>
> Until the eighteenth century, twins were thought to be a curse and were often murdered at birth. However, opinion changed and twins began to be regarded as a sign of great luck and fortune.
>
> It is believed that twins share a soul, and therefore, when one twin dies, a doll

needs to be carved to house the surviving
twin's partial soul. This is thought to keep
the balance of the soul intact and to keep
the living twin from venturing into the
Underworld to retrieve her other half. It is
believed that great misfortune will befall a
family if the doll is neglected or mistreated.

I sat and stared at the screen for several moments,
trying to make sense of what I'd read. The most troub-
ling part was that Ibeji dolls were created to keep the
living twin from venturing into the Underworld to re-
unite with her other half. Except I'd ventured into the
Place-in-Between and found Jade *because* of Lola's Ibeji
doll. I searched a bit more, but could find no information on the consequences of a surviving twin actually
retrieving her other half from the Underworld.

I glance over at Jade now; she's sound asleep beside me,
her seatbelt rising and falling with each shallow breath.
The sunlight hits the paper-thin skin of her eyelids, making the delicate blue veins there visible. There are still dark
circles under her eyes, despite the massive amount of
sleep she's been getting. In fact, she only stayed awake this
morning long enough to push around a pile of scrambled
eggs and take a couple of bites of buttered toast.

"You girls certainly love your sleep," Lola says as she
puts on an upbeat Brazilian tune. The sound of rhyth-
mic drumming fills the car.

"I don't think Jade loves sleeping," I say flatly. "All you
need to do is look at her to see she's actually really sick."

Lola shakes her head. "Don't worry your beautiful heart about her," she says. "After all Jade's been through, she's bound to be in some shock."

"How do you know what she's been through?" I ask. My voice is sharper than intended. "Mom and I don't even know what really happened to Jade since she was gone. And I'm not worried in my heart; I'm worried in my soul."

This time I'm not imagining it; Lola's grip on the steering wheel tightens.

"Jasmine, what has gotten into you?" Mom asks. From the tone in her voice, it's clear she's not pleased with me.

"Nothing," I say. "Sorry, Lola. I guess I'm bitchy because I didn't sleep much last night."

"Language," Mom warns. She turns in her seat again and gives me a stern look.

"Apology accepted," Lola says. "This is a very emotional time for everyone. Especially Jade. That's why I'm so glad Sandra was generous enough to let us stay in her country home. Wait until you see it. It's impossible not to relax there."

"I'm sure it will be great," I say with forced enthusiasm. "Is your friend going to be there?"

"Sandra will be in and out. It's hard for her to get much time at home these days. She's very much in demand."

I found out this morning that Lola's friend, and our host, is the famous environmental scientist, Sandra Smith. You'd have to live under a rock to not know who she is; the fact that she's Canadian is pretty cool. She's really involved in trying to find ways to reverse climate change. She was mentored by Dr. David Suzuki before he died. Lola says Sandra's working her way up in politics because there's been a big public push for her to run for prime minister in a few years. It would be great to finally have a female leading our country, and it would be even cooler if I could say I stayed at her house.

I wonder why Lola never told us they were such good friends. It's just one more thing she's kept secret.

We turn up another road; this one is unpaved and heavily lined with trees. I think we're somewhere near Muskoka, but I'm not sure.

"Anyway, this should be a nice break from that awful school you've had to go to," Lola says.

"It's actually not that bad," I say. "I guess I got used to the weirdness."

This morning I got a message from Ms. Samson. She said they were aware I was leaving and to keep in touch, especially if anything strange started to happen, or if I sensed any danger. Obviously she and Raphael have been talking.

"She's met some really nice friends there, including a cute boy," Mom says, turning around and giving me a big smile and a wink. She looks so young again, so healthy.

Raphael's responsible for that, I think to myself.

Last night, after I looked up the information about the Ibeji doll, I searched for angels named Raphael. Mom was pretty religious until Jade's disappearance, and she took us to church every Sunday when we were growing up, so I know some people believe angels exist. After Jade disappeared, Mom never mentioned church or God or anything like that again. I understood why, even though I was only a kid, because the day Jade disappeared was the day I also stopped believing in God or guardian angels or anything like that. At first I thought the demons I saw in the days and weeks following Jade's disappearance were around because I'd turned my back on God. Then Mom took me to a therapist who made me believe all of it was in my head, and that the visions I was having, and the monsters I was seeing, were just part of my post-traumatic stress.

Now I know the truth.

Raphael is, according to what I read last night, the angel of healing, which explains a lot: Mom getting better, Mr. Jackson's dog, and Lily being brought back from the brink of death.

An angel. That would also explain him being practically everywhere I am, including the Place-in-Between. I guess it's also why he knows so much about me, about Seers, about everything.

And I think it's also the reason I'm not supposed to be able to read his thoughts, and why he was so upset when I did.

"Jasmine? Lola's asked you a question," Mom says.

I snap back to what's going on in the car. "Oh," I say. "Sorry. I guess I was kind of daydreaming."

Lola nods and laughs. It's that deep, belly laugh I used to love so much. Now I can't help but question its genuineness.

"I was asking who this boy is, and if it's a romantic thing."

Something tells me not to answer, that it's best if Lola knows as little as possible.

"It's nothing," I say, casually. "Actually, we had a huge blowout yesterday, so I'd really rather not talk about it if you don't mind."

I swear Lola's examining me via the rear-view mirror.

"Completely understandable," she says, though I know she's lying because what she's thinking is something totally different. She's believes he's somehow involved in Jade's return, though she's not sure how. He's too young to be a Protector, so she's left feeling a bit confused, which I find myself taking some pleasure in.

We pull into a laneway, and a house comes into view. Finally we're here. The conversation ends as we unpack the car.

The house is gorgeous and completely environmentally friendly. It's like we're staying in someone's designer science project. Sandra Smith comes out and greets us. She's yoga-bunny thin with a thick mane of red hair. Though it's clear she's getting ready to leave on another trip, she takes the time to show us around, explaining the unique features of the house.

I'm impressed but continue to keep on my toes. I can't let my guard down. Raphael warned me about becoming relaxed.

"The house is completely solar and wind powered," Sandra explains, flashing me a toothy smile. Everything about her, other than the flaming hair, is white: her skin, her teeth — even her eyes are the lightest blue I've ever seen. I wonder if she's albino. "You'll find the automated blinds close and open according to the position of the sun at different times of the day. Also, all of our water is supplied by a rainwater harvesting system."

I watch Jade nod slowly in response. Her eyes are

closing even as we stand in the centre of the living room with our suitcases in hand.

"Someone looks like she could use an afternoon nap," Sandra says, nodding toward Jade.

"I'll show her to her room," Lola says, grabbing Jade's suitcase. There's no protest from my sister.

Sandra watches them disappear up the stairs.

"I forgot to mention that my assistant, Derek, will be able to help you with anything you need," Sandra says, refocusing her attention on Mom and me. "Just let Lola know, and he'll be here within a few hours." She runs a hand through her hair, and I notice this cool ring she has on. It's bulky and silver and has the Star of David on it. I'm guessing she's Jewish.

"I don't know how we can ever thank you enough," Mom says. Her voice wavers, and when I look over, her eyes are shiny with tears.

"It's nothing you need to thank me for," Sandra replies. She walks over and puts an arm around Mom. "I'm more than happy to help out Lola. We're very indebted to each other."

She glances at me. "Do you have a video phone with you, Jasmine?"

What a weird question. Of course I do. I nod.

"Well, we have a universal, solar-powered charger just inside the kitchen. Feel free to use it tonight."

"Thanks," I say. I'm eager to go, now. I don't like having Jade out of my sight this long, and just remembered I'm supposed to send a text to Ms. Samson to let her know where we are.

Sandra's own phone beeps just as we hear a car pull up. I glance out the window. A Jeep with dark-tinted windows pulls up to the house.

"Derek's timing is always spot on," Sandra says with a laugh. "I'm sorry to have to dash off like this, but I'm needed back in Ottawa. We're trying to pass legislation to close our borders as quickly as possible."

"But won't that mean hundreds of thousands of people, if not millions, will end up dying in the crisis zones?" I ask.

Sandra stops and looks me directly in the eye. "We don't have the resources to sustain any further growth in our population, Jasmine. And some of the people we've already let in seem to think it's perfectly acceptable to bomb our public transportation systems as a means of expressing their anger at what's happening back in their homelands. Do you think that's okay?"

"Well, no," I say, a little taken aback. "I was on the subway during the bombing, so I totally don't think it's okay, but it also doesn't seem right to just let innocent people die."

Sandra nods. "I understand. But tough times call for tough decisions. We've done this to ourselves. Humans … the most destructive species ever. We've ruined our biosphere — the Earth — and overpopulated ourselves. What we really need is another flood, like in Noah's time, to induce a sharp population decline. That would take care of everything quite nicely."

There's nothing I can say back. This woman is nuts. Staying here is beginning to feel like a very bad idea.

Raphael's warning about me being careful while we're away from the city plays in my mind. I look over at Mom.

A sharp horn blast fills the air. Sandra heads toward the door.

"Derek's getting impatient," she says, picking up her suitcase. "I know this is hard to fully comprehend, Jasmine. If people had listened years ago, especially our leaders, we wouldn't be in this mess. But we are. And, if we want any of the human population to survive, we're going to have to make some hard choices."

The horn sounds again, and Sandra hurries out the door, giving Mom and me a brief wave as she leaves.

As soon as the door closes, Mom walks over and sits down on the sofa.

"This is such luxury," she says, looking around the room. I follow her gaze as she marvels at the large, stone fireplace that only uses peat for fuel. There are several Group of Seven paintings on the walls. We had to study them in art class. I think they just look like a bunch of colourful rocks and squiggly trees.

"I'm going to see how Jade is and drop my bag off upstairs," I say. Though it's great to see Mom so relaxed, I can't feel the same way.

The upstairs hallway is a sea of sunlight thanks to the mainly glass ceiling. I'm not really certain which room I'm supposed to be staying in, but I am going to make sure Jade and I are together. The second door to my right is slightly ajar, so I walk over and push it open.

Lola's back is to me. She's leaning over the bed, unpacking her suitcase. The room is large and airy. I watch for a moment as she lays a pile of neatly folded T-shirts on the turquoise duvet cover of her bed.

A few seconds later I reach out and knock on the door.

Lola straightens her back and turns around. She smiles widely at me, and, for a moment, I want everything to be back the way it was before when I believed she loved us as much as her own family.

"Jasmine, why are you knocking at my door? Don't you know you don't need permission to come into my room?"

I shrug. "Just being polite," I say.

"Such a good girl. Don't you want to get yourself settled? You and Jade are next door. I've put her to sleep in there. Wasn't even able to unpack, she was so tired. Poor thing."

"I'll unpack her stuff," I say through gritted teeth. "I guess I'll see you downstairs in a bit."

Lola smiles. "We need to take a walk on the grounds. I'll show you the beehives and the gardens. You'll be amazed."

After all I've seen and been through lately, it will take a lot more than a few bees and some vegetables to amaze me, but I nod with forced enthusiasm anyway.

I turn to leave, and that's when I see her pull out the Ibeji doll and set it on her nightstand. My heart begins to thump rapidly as she takes out a soft cloth and gently wipes the doll, as though it's a newborn baby that's just been bathed.

The doll is here, just as Raphael said it would be. Now I need to find a way to destroy it.

As soon as I'm inside my room with the door securely shut, I take out my phone and send a text to Ms. Samson.

CHAPTER 27

The grounds of the house really are incredible. Everything is lush and green, despite the intense heat we've been having for most of the last few years. Mom, Lola, and I stroll around the nearly two acres of land slowly, taking it all in. I can't help but wonder if there's a team of gardeners and landscapers hiding somewhere in the bushes. Every last piece of grass is immaculately cared for. There's no way Sandra Smith is doing this by herself, especially with her crazy schedule.

We're approaching the beehives when we hear the crunching sound of tires on the drive outside the house, followed by the beep of a car horn.

Lola frowns. "It sounds like someone's here," she says, wiping at a drop of sweat slowly making its way down the side of her neck.

"Maybe Sandra forgot something," Mom says.

"Doubt it," Lola says, turning toward the house. "That woman is the most organized person on the face of this Earth."

We round the corner of the house, and I smile as soon as I see who is waiting for us. Ms. Samson, Lily, and Cassandra are leaning against the hood of a parked car. I have no idea how they got here so quickly.

"Hello, Jasmine," Ms. Samson says as we walk up. "I hope it's okay that we popped by. We're just on our way to go camping." She turns to Lola and Mom. "A bit of a school trip. All the girls are staying at a camp just north of here. The heat in the city right now is too oppressive."

I give the three of them big hugs. "That's amazing. It's so good to see you. Mom, Lola," I say, turning around. "This is my teacher, Ms. Samson, and my friends, Lily and Cassandra."

Mom smiles. "So I finally get to meet Lily and Cassandra," she says, walking over and warmly embracing both of them. "I don't know how to thank you enough for going to the hospital with Jade."

Lola hangs back a bit. She's wary of our visitors and doesn't completely believe their story about camping. I don't blame her; it wasn't the best lie I've ever heard.

One of the back doors of the car opens and Mina appears. She slams the door behind her and stretches, reaching her long, thin arms high above her head to tie back her hair in a loose bun.

"I was boiling in there," she says irritably. "When are we leaving? I'd like to put up a tent before sundown."

I raise an eyebrow at Ms. Samson. Why would she bring Mina here? As if I don't have enough to worry about, now I also have to put up with possibly the most annoying, bitchy person on the planet.

"You really must stay and have a late lunch with us," Mom says. "The least I can do to is feed you a big meal before you go off to only campfire-cooked meals."

Ms. Samson looks over at the girls. Both Lily and Cassandra nod enthusiastically, encouraging her to accept Mom's invitation. Mina crosses her bony arms in front of her chest and glares straight ahead.

"If you're sure it's no trouble …" Ms. Samson begins, glancing uncertainly at Mom.

"Not at all," Mom says. "It's okay, isn't it, Lola? I should've asked."

Lola grins. "Of course. If these girls had anything to do with bringing our Jade back to us, we need to feed them like queens." She turns and waves us toward the house. Except, I know that's the last thing she wants to do. She's wondering how they found us and why they're really here.

Cassandra gives me a sideways glance; she's also just read Lola's thoughts.

After an amazing meal of beans and rice and a fresh salad of dandelion greens, Lily and I go upstairs to check on Jade.

I gently push the door open. The shutters have closed on this side of the house to keep the late afternoon sun out, so I turn on a lamp that's sitting on the dresser. The bulb casts a soft glow over the room. Jade is still under the duvet cover, her long, dark hair spilling over the pillow. Her laboured breathing fills the room.

"How long has she been like this?" Lily whispers, walking into the room behind me.

"She's gotten weaker and weaker since the day we came home," I say, keeping my voice low, though I doubt anything less than a drum and bass party would wake Jade now. "The sleeping has been constant today. She says she's dying."

"What?" Lily says, shocked. "That can't be. She was hardly hurt in the accident. Why does she think that?"

"I can't explain right now," I reply, walking over and sitting down on the edge of the bed. Jade's skin is so pale, it seems almost bloodless. "But she's right. If I don't do something very soon, I think we're are going to lose her." My voice wavers on the last word, and I bite my bottom lip very hard to force back my tears.

"Girls?" It's Mom. She's standing in the doorway, her face full of concern. "She's still asleep?"

"Yeah," I say with false optimism. "I think she's just recovering from the shock of everything. You know, being back and the subway accident. Or maybe it's just a really bad flu."

Mom frowns. "Maybe," she says, doubt edging her voice. "We're going to resume our walk. Gillian ... I mean, Ms. Samson, wants to see the grounds before heading off. Why don't both of you join us?"

I don't like the idea of leaving Jade on her own in the house again, but know that it will seem strange if I don't join everyone on the walk. Reluctantly, I get up from the bed and follow Lily and Mom out of the room, carefully closing the door behind us.

I desperately want to talk to Ms. Samson to find out why they're here, especially with Mina. It's pretty obvious the entire camping-slash-field trip thing is a big excuse, but I don't know whether to feel relieved that other Seers are here, or worried that it means Jade and I are in major danger.

Mina sighs heavily every few minutes to exaggerate her annoyance at having to walk around with us. I grit my teeth and try to ignore her. Lily and Cassandra walk beside me. From the slightly pained expressions on their faces, I can tell they want to ask me questions about Jade and what's happening. I wish there was somewhere we could go and talk, but Lola keeps glancing over as she gives us the tour. She's keeping her on eye on me, which is fine with me because I don't trust her much anymore either.

"I need to go to the bathroom," Mina says to no one in particular.

I don't say anything in response; she can go behind some bush for all I care. Mom looks at me. I stare at the ground, pretending not to notice.

"Jasmine," Mom says, impatience edging into her voice. If there's one thing she doesn't tolerate, it's bad manners. I'm going to hear it about this once everyone leaves.

"Yes?" I arch an eyebrow questioningly at her.

"Take your friend back to the house and show her where the bathroom is, please."

Mina smirks. I wish I could pound that grin right off her face with my fist. Instead, I grit my teeth and smile at Mom.

"Sure. Be right back."

As soon as we're out of earshot, Mina turns to me. The smartass grin is gone. It's been replaced with an expression I've never seen on Mina's face before: concern.

"When we get to the house, you need to take Jade out of there, and then, no matter what, don't come back in. Promise me."

I stare at her in disbelief. What is she talking about?

"Jade's asleep," I say. "She's not feeling well, and I'm not moving her anywhere, thanks very much."

"I know what's happening. Ms. Samson filled me in. That's why we're here. Jade doesn't have much time, but I think you already know that. Twins sense these things, don't we?"

My face grows hot. I feel betrayed by Ms. Samson. Why would she tell Mina what's happening to Jade? And why bring her here? After all, she's a Seer with a dead twin, which means her powers are limited at best.

"Don't be stupid about this, Jasmine. They'll be back from touring around this place soon, and then it will be too late. Just do it, okay? The Seers need you and Jade to be strong. Terrible things are on the horizon."

Her words echo Raphael's, but I trust Mina about as much as I'd trust Hitler. Yet, the desperation in her eyes makes me feel I need to go along with what she's saying. Besides, I can't turn down any offer of help for Jade. Not at this point.

"I know about the doll," she says, interrupting my thoughts. "It needs to be destroyed. It needs to be destroyed so Jade can live. And for you to be whole."

And that's when I realize exactly what she's planning to do.

She smiles at me, knowing I've just read her mind.

"All right," I say. "But if you screw this up … I'll personally kill you."

"I think you and I both know that won't be necessary," she says quietly.

I nod. "Thanks," I say as we continue to walk toward the house. It's all I can manage, and even then the word sticks uncomfortably in my throat.

Jade's still asleep when I enter her room, and it takes a few minutes of gentle shaking and prodding from me before she fully wakes up. Her lips are dry, with little bits of skin hanging off them like loose roof shingles. I grab the glass of water Mom placed on the nightstand and pass it to her. Her hands shake as she gulps it down.

"We've got to go outside for a few minutes," I say, helping her sit up. The way her breath rattles around in her chest scares me.

Jade waves me away. "Too tired," she says weakly.

I wrap a flannel blanket from the foot of the bed around Jade's shoulders.

"Too bad," I say, lifting her off the bed and pulling her left arm around my shoulder. She's surprisingly light. How could she lose so much weight in just a few days? "I promise we won't be long, but this is important."

She doesn't protest as we stumble down the stairs and out the door together. I have no idea where Mina is. There's a gazebo in the far corner of the front lawn. That's likely as far as we're going to get. Jade's fading fast and her weight is becoming too much for me to support.

As soon as we sit down, I smell it. Smoke.

"Oh my God, Jazz," Jade whispers. She's looking at something over my shoulder. "The house."

I swivel to look. There's a thick plume of black smoke rising from one of the bedroom windows on the second floor.

The house is on fire.

CHAPTER 28

Lola's screams rip apart the heavy afternoon air like gunshots as she and Mom run toward the house. Jade's eyes widen, but she doesn't move from her slumped position on the gazebo bench. I watch, frozen, as the glass in one of the windows bursts, sending embers sailing up into the sky like tiny fireflies. Mina's still in there. I make a mental note of which room the fire is coming from. If I'm remembering right, it's the bedroom Lola was going to stay in.

As they get closer to the house, I see that Mom's face is a mask of panic, and realize she still thinks Jade's inside. I stand up.

"We're here!" I shout, waving my hands in the air. "Over here. Jade's with me."

Ms. Samson looks over, grabs Mom's arm, and points.

Relief washes over Mom's face. Everyone heads in our direction, except Lola.

Mom reaches us first and throws her arms around us. She's sobbing, her chest violently rising and falling as she clutches us close.

"Thank God you're both safe," she whispers.

I struggle from her grasp just in time to see Lola enter the house.

The doll. She's going after the doll. Flames lick at the side of the house now and crawl their way up onto the reclaimed wood shingles of the roof. There must be a fire station around here somewhere, but likely it's volunteer and not exactly around the corner.

What Lola's doing is suicide. There's no way she'll make it to the second floor, let alone to the doll. The flames will have consumed it by now. Consumed it and Mina, unless she managed to escape.

I look over at Jade. She's still listless, like a rag doll in Mom's arms. Shouldn't she be improving if the doll has been destroyed?

And, if Lola truly realized the importance of that doll, would she have pulled it out in front of me when she unpacked? Would she have just left it unprotected in her room while all of us went outside? In fact, would she have been so careless as to have dropped it on our kitchen floor in the first place? Or did part of her want me to find it?

Despite having my world turned inside out and upside down over the last week or so, it's still hard for me to believe that Lola would ever purposefully hurt either me or Jade.

I need to get her out of there. She's going to get killed.

Before I can talk myself out of it, I'm running, ignoring the protests from behind me, ignoring the fact that

I'm breaking the promise I made to Mina. The ground bounces up and down in front of me like a trampoline as I run. Glass shatters in the window beside the room where the fire started. The flames are spreading fast.

Smoke fills my lungs as soon as I enter the house, so I drop to the floor and begin to crawl. There's no way Lola's going to make it to the doll; I can feel the heat radiating from the floor above me. And I'm right. Through the smoky haze, I see Lola lying slumped on the stairs to the second floor. She didn't even make it to the third step.

Keeping as low as I can, I make my way over to her. From outside, there's the sound of approaching sirens.

Lola's eyes are half-closed when I reach her, and she seems to be on the brink of unconsciousness.

I shake her shoulders. "Lola!"

She murmurs, opens her eyes a bit wider, and coughs violently several times.

"Jasmine … I'm sorry. I did it for Femi. I had to make a choice …" Another fit of coughing stops her from finishing her sentence.

This is not the time to have a conversation. My eyes are stinging from the smoke. It's getting thicker by the second. Tears pour down my cheeks. There's an enormous cracking sound from somewhere above us. The sirens are closer now. I doubt they have many, if any fire fighting drones out here.

"I need to get us out of here," I say. "We don't have much time." The smoke is choking me now; it's like a fist closing around my lungs.

I move Lola so that the back of her head is against

my chest. Then I kneel, grab her under the armpits, and begin to drag her off the stairs. She's heavy, much heavier than I expected, and a sudden rush of light-headedness washes over me like an ocean wave.

"I thought at least I could keep you safe. I'm sorry.... You don't know how sorry I am," Lola murmurs, her voice cracking with emotion.

"It's okay. We need to just get out of here," I say, finishing my sentence with a fit of coughing.

Dragging her is too much. My lungs spasm from the smoke; I can't catch my breath. Dizziness washes over me, and for a moment the room lurches sickeningly, causing me to drop Lola to the floor. She doesn't react: she's nearly unconscious now. I lie on my stomach, sucking at the air like a fish that's been flung out of water, desperate for any last bit of oxygen I can get. The darkness is closing in.

Mina was right; I shouldn't have come back in here.

"If I didn't let them take Jade, Femi would've died ... but I made sure she didn't die. I didn't want her to die."

For a moment, the world freezes. Lola's eyelids are fluttering like butterfly wings as she tries to regain consciousness. "What did you just say?" I ask, my voice trembling, but it's too late, she's not responsive at all, even when I shake her.

I should leave her. She just admitted she let Jade be taken so that Femi could live. Her job was to protect my sister and me. Instead, if what she said is true, she allowed Jade's abduction. She basically sacrificed my sister.

The familiar rage is back. My body shakes with it. I'm going to leave Lola here. Let her feel the kind of fear Jade must've felt all these years, trapped in the Place-in-Between. I hope she regains consciousness before the flames take her, so she can experience the burn.

I begin to pull myself along on my belly, snakelike, toward the door, trying to ignore the part of me that's screaming to go back and get Lola. The open door is just a few metres away now, the light from outside guiding me like a beacon. I've got enough energy to make it.

And that's when I look back over my shoulder at Lola lying motionless on the wood floor. If I leave her here to die, that makes me no better than her. It would be like murder. But, more than anything else, if Lola dies, it will break Mom's heart.

I turn, crawl back to Lola, and put both my hands under the fleshy part of her upper back. My eyes sting from the heat and smoke, causing tears to run down my cheeks.

"Come on," I whisper. "Help me out here."

And that's when I see it. A dark shadow moves toward me, emerging from the smoke, getting closer and closer. I open my mouth to scream, but nothing comes out. A few moments later, the darkness swallows me.

CHAPTER 29

All I smell is smoke. When I open my eyes, the light is blinding, and I immediately close them again.

"Jasmine. Can you hear me?" It's Jade. Her hand touches my shoulder, and she shakes me gently, encouraging me to open my eyes again.

This time I shield my eyes against the light. Faces loom above me. Mom's here and Jade, as well as Ms. Samson, Lily, and Cassandra. Everyone is looking at me with this weird mixture of concern and relief. I open my mouth and try to ask where I am, but all that comes out is a strangled, toad-like croak followed by a fit of coughing. The inside of my chest feels like it's been rubbed raw with sandpaper.

A nurse suddenly appears and slips a plastic mask over my nose and mouth. Almost immediately my chest loosens, and I feel better.

Ms. Samson leans in close. "You tried to save Lola, and the firefighters saved you. But going into that house wasn't supposed to be an option. We need you to control your emotions better, Jasmine."

She's annoyed with me. I know my actions were driven by emotion, but I couldn't just leave Lola.

Jade perches on my bed, her eyes fill with tears of happiness. She looks good; there's colour in her cheeks and energy in her movements. It worked. Mina destroyed the doll and freed Jade's soul, the other half of my soul.

"I feel okay now," she whispers, giving me a massive hug.

I lift the mask off my face for a moment. "Is Lola all right? What about Mina?" I ask.

There's no need for anyone to answer. Even if I couldn't read thoughts, the look on their faces tells me all I need to know: I was the only one who made it out of the house alive. Jade straightens and fixes her eyes on the floor.

I put the mask back on and breathe deeply.

In the smoke, just before I'd blacked out, someone was walking toward me. At first I thought it was a firefighter arriving. But it wasn't. It was my guardian angel, Raphael. He saved me.

CHAPTER 30

I'm sitting with Mr. Khan at a table in the cafeteria, pushing food aimlessly around on my plate. Though it's only been a couple of weeks since the fire at Sandra Smith's house, things have changed so quickly it feels like ancient history.

"We didn't realize Mina's mother was unwell," Mr. Khan says, watching me mix a spoonful of salsa into my rice. "But she became increasingly distraught about her daughters' abilities to read minds, and decided the girls were possessed." His face darkens. "We should've seen the signs: the sudden religious fervor, the way she started to isolate the girls by keeping them home from school…."

I stop playing with my food and look up at him.

Mom sent me to a therapist after Jade disappeared because of my insistence on seeing monsters. But that wasn't the only reason she sent me. I haven't thought about it in a long time, but I was also predicting things, and so was Jade in the year or so leading up to her disappearance. They were mainly just little things, like knowing Lola waiting for us at home when we weren't expecting her to visit, or a surprise package arriving in the mail. Still, it must've been pretty unnerving, if not absolutely scary, for Mom.

"Mina was always strong-willed and impatient. She was the first-born twin. Like you." He pauses for a moment before continuing. "That morning, when everything finally came to a head, her mother, Lucy, tried to get her in the car, but Mina refused, threw a massive tantrum, and ran away. She must've known what was going to happen. So I was called to go and look for Mina. Lucy said she couldn't do it because she had an important meeting to get to."

"How long did you know Mina?" I ask, taking a sip of my juice.

"Since her birth, though she and her family didn't always know me," Mr. Khan says. "I kept an eye on her until I felt it was time to become a part of her life. A Seer's power develops around the time of puberty." He smiles wistfully. "Mina's mother was an educational assistant. I made sure she was assigned to work in my classroom, when it became time for me to take a more hands-on approach to being Mina's Protector."

I nearly choke. "You were Mina's Protector? But you're a man. I thought Protectors are always female."

He nods. "I was born in a female body, Jasmine, but never felt female. Does that disqualify me as a Protector? Certainly not. It also makes me the most unique Protector yet," he says. "Anyway, because Mina ran away that day, her life was spared. The important meeting Lucy couldn't be late for turned out to be driving herself and Mina's twin, Melody, into the concrete buttress of an overpass. They both died instantly."

We sit in silence for the next few minutes. I can't imagine what it must've been like for Mina to lose her mom and her twin in such a terrible way.

"Ms. Samson was horrible to Mina the first day of class," I say, finally breaking the quiet. "Why?"

"She was trying to make Mina get past her anger and guilt about what happened. Negative emotions are dangerous, and hers were strong. Much like yours."

Now it's my turn to look down at an imaginary spot on the table. Maybe Mina and I had more in common than I cared to admit.

"Can I ask you a question?"

Mr. Khan nods. "About Mina?"

"About Mina," I say, chewing nervously on the tip of my plastic straw. "Why did she go in and start the fire at Sandra Smith's? She must've known it was suicide."

"The doll needed to be destroyed," Mr. Khan replies. "You knew that, but it would've been too dangerous for you to attempt to do it. Jade had a finite amount of time left. There are people that would've done anything to protect that doll."

"People like Lola?" I ask.

He nods again. "Lola. Sandra Smith. Anyone who realized how strong you and Jade are."

I raise an eyebrow at him. "How strong we are?"

"As Seers, you're special. There are many things you'll learn when the time is right. As for Mina, she volunteered herself. She realized that a Seer with half a soul is vulnerable, and that it might be hard for us to protect her in the future. I think it was her way of redeeming herself. A way to lift the guilt of her sister's death off her conscience."

"But what her mother did wasn't her fault," I protest. "She shouldn't have had to die."

"Just as it wasn't your fault Jade was taken," Mr. Khan says quietly. "Nor was it my fault that I couldn't prevent Melody's death. After all, I was supposed to be her Protector."

We sit for a moment together. What Mina did blows my mind. She gave her life for Jade ... and for me.

Mr. Khan clears his throat. "I'd like to take on the role of Protector for you and Jade. If you'll have me," he says. "We know there's a definite rift somewhere between our world and the Place-in-Between. Demons are spilling through. The threat to Seers is great, perhaps greater than ever before. We need to be ready for battle, but first we need to find out why this is happening."

He finishes speaking and begins tracing invisible circles on the tabletop with his finger, waiting for my answer.

"Of course I want you to be my Protector," I say, reaching across the table and putting my hand on top of his. It's an odd thing to do, but somehow it feels right. "And I'm sure Jade will want you, to be, too."

He smiles, but the relief is only temporary. Worry immediately clouds his face again.

"Should I be terrified about all of this rift stuff?" I ask.

"Yes," he answers immediately.

"Don't beat around the bush or anything," I retort, taking another sip of my drink.

"It's very serious, Jasmine. We've gathered as many Seers from across the globe as possible together, but things are moving more quickly than anyone could've predicted. Our borders are closing, and millions could die. There's talk that rather than just being a dark period in time, this could be the beginning of the final prophecy."

"Final prophecy?" I say. "I take it that's not so good either."

"No, it's not. If that is what we're truly faced with." Mr. Khan straightens up. "Right now we have Seers to train, so you'll be ready for all of this if and when it happens." He pushes back his chair and stands up. "You've come a long way from being the angry girl I met at the beginning of this school year, but there's still quite a journey ahead."

"Thanks," I say, not really sure if I should take Mr. Khan's comment as a compliment. "Can I ask you one more thing?"

He nods. "Sure."

I chew nervously on my bottom lip, hesitating for a moment. "Do you know what happened to Raphael? Is he ever coming back? I kind of thought he was my Protector."

Mr. Khan regards me for a moment. "Raphael and his brothers will always be with us when the time is right. You do know he's not like us, don't you, Jasmine?"

I bob my head up and down. My face is hot. "I know," I mumble.

"Then you know you mustn't think of him as human. You mustn't think of him as you would other boys your age. And he's not a Protector. He can guard and guide, but cannot change the course of events."

I'm getting a lecture from Mr. Khan on who I should and shouldn't date. I feel sick to my stomach.

"I know," I say, irritation edging my voice. "I just kind of miss him. Is that okay?"

"No, actually it's not," Mr. Khan says. "Not at all. Take my advice, Jasmine. Focus on the Seers and the threat facing us now. If anything were to happen between you and Raphael …" He trails off.

But he doesn't need to finish. I've read his thoughts. It would be chaos. It could mean the demise of the human race. It must never happen.

As I watch Mr. Khan walk away, I throw my bag over my shoulder and decide whatever challenges lay ahead — demonic or otherwise — I'll be ready.

ACKNOWLEDGEMENTS

Thank you to Mum and Dad for your love and support. A huge thank you to my editor, Shannon Whibbs; to my agent, Amy Tompkins, at the Transatlantic Literary Agency; and to Kirk Howard, publisher at Dundurn. Thank you to both the Ontario and Canadian Arts Council for their generous financial support in the creation of this work. Most of all, thank you to my students — both past and present — at Nelson Mandela Park PS and Lord Dufferin PS for teaching me about resilience and courage.